NORTH WOODS
POACHERS

Max Elliot Anderson

Comfort PUBLISHING

North Woods Poachers

First printing
Book cover design by Colin Kernes
ISBN: 978-1-936695-05-8

Published by Comfort Publishing, LLC
www.comfortpublishing.com

Printed in the United States of America

Dedicated to

**Judge
Joseph G. McGraw**
a man of Justice

Chapter 1

There was no escaping it. The day had come, and there was absolutely nothing Andy Washburn could do to change it.

Every summer it was the same story. His family, along with his cousins and their parents, made the same trip to the same place to do the same thing year after year.

"Not this time!" Andy defiantly declared right out loud as he stuffed the last clothes he needed into two large duffel bags. "This trip is going to be different."

He didn't even get to pack real suitcases like other normal families when they went on vacation. It felt more like getting ready for a survival trip than something fun. Still, he continued packing.

Andy's attitude was odd in a way because he was the most athletic member of the two families. He should be the one person in the group who would love the outdoors. His father liked to remark that his son was nothing but muscle and bone.

At school, Andy was one of the best at any

sport he tried.

This was in direct contrast to his cousin. CJ didn't like sports at all. His favorite activity was playing around with anything electronic. Since his father owned a computer solutions company, CJ had all the "toys" anyone could imagine.

Andy and CJ's birthdays were only three days apart. Just before school started again in the fall they'd both be twelve years old.

At least I know CJ and Jessie have to go too, Andy thought . . . not that it helped much.

Sarah, Andy's nine-year-old sister, and Jessica, CJ's sister, could practically be twins. Each had dark brown hair and the greenest eyes. Like their brothers, the girls were almost exactly the same age. Both girls had long hair that they wore in ponytails nearly every day.

The boys were best friends, and so were the girls.

Sarah came into his room. "Are you still packing?"

"What if I am?"

"Just wondering. I've been done for hours. What's taking you so long?"

"I don't feel like going, that's all."

"Are you kidding? We've gone on this trip for as long as I've been alive. Mom said I went one year before I was even born."

"Want a medal?"

"Huh?"

"Never mind. It's just that we drive on the same roads, to the same lake, stay in the same cabins, in the same old Canada. I think when the fish see us coming they say, 'Here come the Washburns,' and then laugh their fins off."

"Well, you know how much Dad loves to fish." Sarah left him so he could finish his packing.

Later, Andy walked into the kitchen downstairs. His mother was busy getting some last things together, and Sarah sat at the table eating toast.

Andy sighed. "We're the only family on our whole street with a fish mailbox, Mom. Do you know how embarrassing that is for a kid my age? Our den looks like a nature show with all those fish hanging on the wall. Sometimes when I walk in there, I think I've fallen under water."

He began to mock, "Every year Dad and Uncle Joe say they're gonna catch Big Wally, the oldest, biggest Walleye in the whole lake. But they never do."

His mother smiled as she reassured, "Someone's going to catch that old fish one day. Remember, they marked him with that bright red tag on his tail."

Andy interrupted, "How could I forget? Dad

keeps the yellowed newspaper picture from the day they did that. He even has to have the number 4112 on his license plate. I think he's obsessed."

"Your Dad's proud of the fish he's caught. I know he'd love to add Big W to his trophy wall."

"I know, but then he turns around and tries to teach me everything he knows about fishing. This time, I'm going to skip the lessons and try to find something else to do."

"Like what?"

"I don't know, but there's gotta be something more fun than fishing all day, every day, for two weeks. And I plan to find it!"

"Can I go with you?" Sarah asked with excitement.

"Why not?" Andy replied. "I was thinking of asking CJ and Jess if they want to come with us, too."

"Kids!" their father called from the den. "Time for a final family meeting before we load up the truck and head out."

"Great," Andy sighed. "I was hoping he might have forgotten the trip this year."

"That's pretty funny," Sarah snickered. "You know this is about the only thing Dad and Mom look forward to all year."

"Don't remind me."

Andy, Sarah, and their mother headed to the

family room. As Andy sat in the recliner, he felt like all those fish hanging on the walls were staring straight at him.

Don't look at me, he thought. It's not my fault you were so dumb you got caught.

Even though Andy's father and his Uncle Joe were brothers, they didn't look at all alike. Andy's father was tall, slim, and worked in a pharmacy. His uncle was short and heavy.

Unfortunately for Andy, the one thing they did have in common, besides having the same father and mother, was their love for fishing. That didn't help Andy at all.

"Your Uncle Joe and Aunt Julie will be here any minute. Are you all packed?"

"I am," Sarah announced proudly.

"Almost," Andy said.

"What's the hold up?"

"Nothin'. I *said* almost."

"All right," Andy's mother began. "This is going to be such a fun trip. Every year as you get older, there are more things we can do together."

That's about the last thing Andy wanted to hear. This was the year he had plans to do less with his family, and here they were expecting more.

Andy's father added, "I talked with my brother this morning, and he told me Aunt Julie, CJ, and Jessie can hardly wait."

Andy's mother worked in a library, and his Aunt Julie managed an office for three eye doctors. Whenever they went on vacation, both moms were transformed into master cooks and bakers. That was something that Andy *did* like about the trip, though he wasn't about to admit it.

Their mother instructed, "Hurry back upstairs, bring down your things, and let's get started."

Andy dragged himself back upstairs as slowly as possible, thinking that might give him just a few extra minutes before starting his boring trip. He hoped his cousin CJ would at least bring along some of his latest computer gear to play with. While that thought was still in his head, he heard the sound of a horn in the front yard. He went to his window and looked out, as if expecting to see something different than what was sitting in the driveway.

Andy's father and Uncle Joe bought exactly the same extended cab pickup trucks, the biggest ones Detroit makes.

They were so huge that Andy thought there should be a ladder to help climb in. Both trucks had custom-made tops to cover the things that were loaded in back. Each truck had double rear tires which were especially important for the last fifty miles of the trip. They also had double gas tanks for maximum driving range.

Loaded for the trip, each truck had a full-sized fishing boat and trailer hitched on behind. Not only were the trucks filled to the gills with clothes, food, and supplies, but the boats were completely loaded too.

I don't know why he has to copy my dad all the time, Andy thought. *At least Uncle Joe's is a different color.*

Sadly, he went back over to his bed, pulled both duffel bags off onto the floor, and began dragging them to the door.

They sounded like double earthquakes as each bag hit every step on the way down the stairs, "Can't you pick those things up?" his mother asked.

"Too heavy," he grunted. "Sorry." Actually, he was happy he'd done something she didn't like since that's the way he felt about this whole trip idea, and, as far as Andy was concerned, his parents didn't seem to care if he was happy about it or not.

Andy helped his father cram the last few things in back of their truck while his mother locked all the doors, checked the windows and timers, set the alarm, and then closed the front door behind her.

That's the end of my freedom, Andy thought.

"Hey," CJ said as he walked up to Andy.

"Here, I brought a couple of radios so we can talk, truck to truck."

"That's a great idea," Andy said. He liked the way his cousin knew about all kinds of electronic gadgets. At least that kept things a little more interesting.

"We can use them to tell everyone we need a pit stop, or gas, or something," CJ said.

"All right everyone, time to go," Andy's dad announced.

The two families piled into their trucks, and the latest installment of the Washburn family adventure was about to begin. Their trip took them almost straight west on Interstate 90. That was another thing Andy thought was boring, just one straight ribbon of road for miles and miles. In South Dakota they'd be turning north on Interstate 29 and head up through Fargo. That would be the first chance for anything exciting to happen.

That's because not far from Fargo, the families would have to pass through the border crossing between the United States and Canada. Andy liked to imagine a time when the guards would stop his dad's truck and find some reason to send the family back home.

Andy's mother collected all kinds of fun things through the year for Andy and Sarah to do along the way. There were some old favorites that had come on every trip before like Travel Battleship, word games, and others. But this year Andy had the radio. He picked it up, turned it on, and called, "Hey, CJ, you there?"

"Yes, I'm here, and I've been here trying to talk to you for the last fifty miles. Where you been?"

"I had mine turned off. You know . . . to save the batteries."

"Don't worry about that. They're rechargeable. You can keep the thing on all the way to Canada and back if you want to."

That was CJ all right. He was always thinking.

"So, you guys tired of sittin' yet?"

"I sure am. I think this trip gets longer every time."

Andy's mother turned and smiled back at him.

"How's it going in your battle wagon?" Andy asked.

"My mom's asleep already, and Jessie is right behind her."

Sarah sat up a little straighter in her seat, so Andy wouldn't think she was tired.

"I brought a bunch of wireless stuff to try out this time," CJ continued.

"Like what?"

"You name it . . . I've probably got one. I had

to leave a few more clothes at home this time around so I'd have room for all the extra stuff."

"So what have you got?"

"I can connect my laptop by satellite so we have the Internet up there this year."

"How can you do that?"

"I'm testing a satellite uplink and a downlink dish system."

Andy laughed. "My Dad might be a couch potato, but you're a mouse potato, CJ."

"I don't get it."

"Your computer . . . you're on it constantly."

"I know, but part of it is to help my dad decide if he likes certain computer products. Plus, I brought a boat load of junk so we can build some stuff if we want to."

"What kind of stuff?"

"We can talk about it later. Hey, was that your dad's fishing boat that just went whizzing past us?"

Andy's dad quickly slowed down and looked out his rear view mirror.

"Just kidding," CJ laughed. "Sorry."

The truck sped up again. Andy keyed his radio and said,

"Guess my dad thought that wasn't very funny."

"Well, I forgot to tell you to use the earplug and

mouthpiece. These conversations are supposed to be private."

"I'll do that. Where's mine?"

"In the pouch with the charger and extra rechargeable batteries."

"Okay, I found it."

"Do you have it connected yet?"

"Yes," Andy assured him.

"Good, because I wanted to ask you something."

"Shoot."

"That's not funny considering where we're going. It's nothing but hunting and fishing in all directions."

"I know. What's your question?"

In a hushed voice his cousin continued, "Tell me if I'm wrong, but it didn't seem to me that you cared all that much about fishing last year. Am I right?"

"I don't hate it. It's just that I'd like to do something else besides only fishing. That's all."

"Same here. So I have an idea."

"Shoo . . . I mean go ahead."

"You and I should be old enough by now that they can trust us to go off on our own once in awhile."

"I'm listening."

"We don't have any idea what's around those

cabins we stay in. Except for the boat dock, the store, and a few float planes that come in, what have we really seen anyway?"

"I thought the same thing while I was packing."

"So," CJ continued, "suppose we go along with fishing the first couple days, like we always have. But this time we ask, real nice of course, if we can do some exploring."

"And see what they say?"

"Yes."

"I'm all for that. Let's talk about it at the next pit stop."

"Roger."

"Who's Roger? This is still Andy."

"It's just radio talk. It means okay."

"You mean some poor kid named Roger is really named okay?"

"Cute, Andy, real cute. I'm gonna catch some winks. Talk to you later . . . out."

Andy's mind was already racing full speed. The very idea that his cousin was thinking the same things he'd thought about was a welcome surprise. What exactly might they find out in those north woods? Just the thought gave him goose bumps.

Chapter 2

Andy wasn't exactly sure when it happened. In fact, he wasn't sure of anything because he had fallen so sound asleep.

His mouth was up against the window, and he'd slobbered on it. CJ's father pulled his truck alongside as Andy's radio crackled, "Hey, Basset Hound, are you dead or what?"

Andy still had his earpiece in. His cousin's voice caused him to jerk, and he hit his head on the window. CJ just started laughing into his radio.

"My dad says he needs to stop for gas. This hog drinks it pretty fast. How's yours doing?"

"Hang on, I'll ask," Andy said in a half slurred voice. "Hey, Dad, do we need gas yet?"

"We could use the stop."

At the next exit, both trucks eased onto the ramp and headed toward a small country road. At the stop sign, they had several choices. Uncle Joe made a right and pulled into the station with the cheapest price. Andy's truck pulled up to a pump across from theirs. While the two dads filled up, Andy and his cousin started planning.

"I think we should fish for the first couple of days like you said," Andy began. "Then we can see about doing a little exploring. I'll even ask my dad ahead of time."

"That's a good idea. Since our families usually have supper together each night, I'll just back you up like it's news to me."

"I like that, and if you think of something, I'll do the same thing."

"What about Sarah and Jessie?" Andy wondered.

"I'd like to ditch 'em, but if they want to come with us, who could blame them?"

A few minutes later the families were back to full speed nearing their turn to the north.

"Dad," Andy began, "how come we always come up here? I mean, we've never taken a trip anywhere else during the summer."

"Tradition," his mother answered. "It's a family tradition."

"I know, but why is that so important?"

"Traditions are things a family can count on and look forward to each year. It gives them a good feeling to know they can always expect certain things."

"Yeah, but fishing in Canada . . . *every* year?"

"So, do you mean to say you don't think traditions are important?" his father asked.

"Kinda."

"Would you like us to stop some of the family things we do?"

"Would that be so bad?"

"Well, then let me see," his mother thought. "What if we stopped celebrating Christmas or your birthday? What if I quit making a turkey dinner at Thanksgiving, too? We could have peanut butter sandwiches on that day."

"Now wait a minute. Some traditions are just more important than the others," Andy protested.

"Oh, and who gets to decide which ones are important and which ones aren't?" his mother asked.

"I see what you mean. No, I like being together as a family. I just wouldn't mind getting to do something different, that's all."

"There are a lot of boys your age who would do almost anything to be sitting where you are right now."

"And I might like to let them, too."

"That's enough discussion about it for now," his father said. "Besides, it's too late to turn back. There's the sign to Fargo now."

Both trucks turned off of Interstate 90, and the digital compass in Andy's truck went from the "W" to the "N."

Why am I not excited? he thought.

"Get on your radio and let Uncle Joe know we'll make a final stop in Grand Forks to gas up one more time and check everything out. After that, it gets a little wilder."

Andy did that. Then he asked, "Does anybody live up in this part of the country?"

"Out here it's mostly farmers. These are wheat fields."

"I don't see farms or anything."

"The Interstate is designed to let us go as fast as possible. Little towns are what used to slow travel down . . . that and the two lane highways."

"Hey, Andy," C J broke in on his earpiece.

"What?"

"What, what?" Andy's mother asked.

"Nothing."

"Who you telling nothing?" C J asked.

"Not you."

"Not who?" his mother and C J asked at the same time.

"I'm talkin' to C J, Mom."

"Who you calling Mom?" CJ asked.

"You want me to switch this thing off?" Andy asked.

"Naw, I'm just goofin' around. My dad says we'll

be in Grand Forks in about an hour. That means we'll cross the border while it's still light."

"Good. I think it would be creepy after dark."

"Me, too. I wonder what they're looking for."

"Whatever it is, I don't think we got any of it."

"I hope not."

The two families didn't stay in motels on the trip. Each brought along a tent and sleeping bags. One thing is certain about their trips to Canada. They were a little on the rough side.

In Grand Forks the trucks again pulled into a service area to gas up, check the tires, see if the boat hitches were still tight, and look for any other problems with the trucks or trailers. Andy remembered that once across the border the road they would be driving on was nothing like the Interstate.

The gas tanks were filled, and everything checked out okay. "Eighty more miles and we'll be in Canada," Andy's dad called out. "Let's saddle up." Soon, truck doors were slamming, and they were back on the road.

It wasn't long before Andy's father announced, "There's, the border."

Andy and his sister tried to look through the split front seats at exactly the same time, and when they did, their heads cracked together.

"Ow," they howled in unison.

"Sorry, Sarah, but you really have a hard head. You know that?"

Andy looked ahead again to see yellow flashing lights.

There were a few trucks with big trailers in one lane and mostly cars in the other. A guard walked to the window of each car as it came to a stop at the line. Uncle Joe's truck was in the lead again. All the other times they had made this crossing, the American guard just had a couple of questions. The Canadian guard had looked at each person and then simply waived them through. But this time, something happened.

"Look, Dad, Uncle Joe has to pull over to the inspection place."

"I know. I wonder what they're looking for."

As Andy's family came to the Canadian guard, the same thing happened to them. The guard looked in at each member of the family, then said, "Pull over for inspection."

Andy's father drove into a parking spot right next to his brother. They looked at each other and shrugged their shoulders. Then Andy noticed something over at another inspection station.

"Those people have all their stuff sitting on the ground," he said. Just then, an inspector opened a panel where the car's spare tire should be. But it wasn't there. Instead, when he reached down, he pulled out a small cage. Andy's father walked over to take a look. After a few minutes, he came back to the truck.

"What was it?" Andy asked.

"They had a crate of wood turtles, but most of them were already dead."

"That's so sad," Sarah said. "What were they doing under there?"

"Those people are poachers."

"What's a poacher?"

"They steal animals and animal parts."

"How come?" Andy asked.

"Because there's big money in it. That's why. They also pulled two trash bags full of eagle feathers out. Those things are worth thousands, but it's illegal to sell them."

"Ill eagle. That's funny, Dad."

"Why are a few turtles and feathers so expensive?" Sarah asked.

"Because anytime something is endangered and people can't get them legally anymore, the price goes up."

An inspector came up to the window holding a clipboard with important-looking forms on it. "What have we got in the back?" he asked.

Andy listened to his father answer. "Household things, food, fishing gear, things like that."

"Anything special to declare?"

"No, sir."

"Mind if I take a look?"

Andy's heart started pounding.

"What's going to happen?" Sarah whispered.

"Shhh," their mother instructed.

"No, sir, go right ahead. We've been making this trip every year as a family. We wouldn't want to do anything wrong."

The guard took another look at Andy's dad. Then he looked over to his mom.

"Do you people have your fishing licenses yet?"

"No. We plan to get them at the store up at Dore Lake, like we always do."

"Dore Lake? Mighty fine fishing up there I hear." The guard checked off a couple things on his form. Then he walked around to the back of the truck. Andy thought it looked like he was writing down their license number. When he came back, Andy's dad asked, "What seems to be the trouble?"

"No trouble. It's just that security's been beefed up all along our borders. We have to take a second look at everything these days, just to make sure."

"Understandable," Andy's father responded.

"Well, you and the other Washburn family are free to go. Enjoy your stay in Canada, and leave a few fish for the rest of us," he joked.

"We will. Thank you."

As the trucks pulled out of the inspection area and onto the main road, Andy had an uneasy feeling. He asked his father, "Are poachers dangerous?"

"The inspector told me many of them are connected to organized crime. Do you know what that is?"

"Sort of."

"To make it really simple, it's a bunch of people that work together to break the law and make a lot of money. It doesn't just happen . . . they plan it."

"How much money is a lot of money?"

"You take those eagle feathers . . . they come from the bald eagle. That's our national bird. The guard told me that people in Europe will pay as much as $50,000 for an Indian headdress if it has eagle feathers on it. But selling one is against the law."

"Whew! How come they don't get caught when they sell something like that?"

"It's the Internet. The Internet has changed everything. With emailing, chat rooms, and auctions, the authorities have their hands full."

"Do you think there are poachers where we're going?"

"Have you seen any the other years we've been

up here?"

"No."

"Well, there you have it then."

That answer didn't sit well with Andy. In fact, he didn't like it at all. It felt like one of those "Because I told you so" kind of answers his parents liked to give sometimes.

Andy settled down in his seat. He thought and thought for the longest time.

Poachers. Wonder if we have any around Dore Lake?

Chapter 3

As they camped that night, Andy couldn't get the idea of poachers out of his thoughts. He wondered what they looked like. Did they hurt other people? Next to their tent was a trailer. The people in there had a television, and right then they were watching the late news.

"And in our crime segment tonight," an announcer began, "we bring you a story of wild animals, poachers, and guns. Last night at around midnight, authorities in Moose Jaw, Saskatchewan, burst into a hideout where they found exotic animals, weapons, and over two million dollars in cash."

Two million, Andy thought.

"Police also arrested five poachers in the raid."

That made Andy sit right up in his sleeping bag. The rest of his family was already asleep but not Andy. Slowly, he opened the screen at the front of the tent and slipped quietly over to where his cousin was sleeping.

"CJ, are you awake?" he whispered.

"Sorta," his cousin whispered back.

"Come on out. We need to talk."

When C J came outside, the two boys went over and sat on a picnic table.

"I just heard the most amazing thing. The cops busted a bunch of poachers right up in Saskatchewan."

"So what?"

"Dore Lake is in Saskatchewan, isn't it?"

"It is?"

"I think so."

"Yeah, but it's a huge place, and my dad reminded me that where we go is fifty miles farther north than the nearest anything."

"I know. That's why so many people come up in float planes . . . but poachers! Man . . . that really scares me."

"If you hear about an accident someplace, does that scare you out of taking a trip like this?"

"Well, no."

"Then I wouldn't worry anymore about poachers. The chances of us seeing one are about as good as our families not making this same trip next year."

"Yeah, you're probably right. Thanks."

"Now go to sleep, will ya?"

"Okay, night."

"And the bed bugs, and all that."

The boys quietly returned to their tents. As Andy crawled into his sleeping bag, he looked over to his sister. She was sleeping so peacefully. *I wonder if she knows anything about the dangerous kinds of people that might be around us at this very minute.* That thought kept him awake for at least another hour.

As they continued on the next morning, their trip took them through parts of Manitoba and on to Saskatchewan. "How much farther, Dad?"

"Around eight hundred miles by my count."

"So we should be pulling in after dark?"

"Oh, I don't think so. Remember, we always camp three times up and three times back."

"That's right, I forgot." Andy got on his radio, "CJ, you on?"

"Do ducks fly?"

"Did you remember we'll camp out again before we get there?"

"Naturally. Don't you remember? The last fifty miles of this trip is up and down all those hills on nothin' but gravel roads. When it rains, forget it."

"That's right. I remember now," Andy said.

"You wouldn't want to hit any moose in the dark would you?"

"No."

"What did you want?" CJ asked.

"You wanna swap seats with my sister at the next gas station?"

"Sure, why not."

"I'll ask."

"Me, too."

A few seconds later CJ came back on. "It's okay in this set of wheels, what about you?"

"Same here."

"I'll bring some of my computer stuff."

"Great."

Their twin trucks continued to power down the Trans-Canadian Highway. In Andy's truck the compass changed from "W" to "NW." He knew when it pointed straight to the "N" again they'd be nearing the end of the line. But these roads weren't like the Interstate at all. Not only were some of them only two lanes, they also passed through small towns with stoplights, stop signs, and traffic. Now he remembered why this part of the trip took so long.

CJ came back on the radio. "Andy, my dad wants to make a gas stop."

"Tell him to eat some tacos and refried beans."

"You should be on late night TV"

"Maybe we ought to try out."

"Yeah, we could start something new called stupid cousin tricks."

"I'll tell my dad."

"About our new show-biz careers?"

"About stopping."

They rolled into a place called Yorktown and found a gas station. While their fathers were filling up, Andy helped his sister move her things into CJ's truck. Then CJ brought some of his computer toys over to Andy's.

"I'm glad we're riding together," Jessica said. "I'm tired of listening to my dad and my brother talk about computers all day."

"We can find some fun games to play. My mom brought a ton." The girls giggled as they walked together toward Uncle

Joe's truck. He and Aunt Julie climbed in as the rest of the Washburns went to theirs.

Andy's father announced, "A couple hundred miles, then we turn straight north."

"It's about time," Andy complained. "I've about worn out every sitting part on my body."

"I did that a long time ago," CJ laughed.

"So, what did you bring for us to play with?"

"My dad is beta testing a new game system. We have two of them, so I've connected them with this cable. Now you and me can go head-to-head and watch our own screens."

"What's the big deal about that? Other games did it years ago."

"Other games?" C J howled. "Man those games were prehistoric. Wait till you see the graphics on these babies!" He powered them up, and the images nearly leaped out of the screens.

"I've never seen anything like this before," Andy gasped. "Where did they come from?"

"Japan . . . where else? That's where all this cool stuff comes from. If people like me give it a good rating, you might be begging your parents for one this Christmas."

"And we expect a big discount, too," Andy's mother joked.

"Sure. Didn't know you were listening. Long as it isn't the five-finger discount. My dad gets enough of those already."

Andy looked at him and wrinkled up his face. "Five-finger discount?"

"Yeah, five-finger discount. Midnight requisition."

"What are you talking about?"

"They steal the stuff, man."

"You could have just said that."

"Come on, let's play."

C J had hockey, football, basketball, NASCAR, and several others. The boys played for the next few hours. When

Andy looked up and began paying attention to the trip, he noticed the compass now read "N."

"Hey Dad, when did we turn?"

"Not long ago, but I think you were about to become champion of the world again. Wouldn't want to disturb the champ."

"Why did you start coming way up here in the first place, Dad?"

"Some friends told us about it. I was looking for a place where we could get away from the rest of the world for a couple weeks. Up here it's quiet. It's safe. Nothing ever happens."

That's what Andy thought, and to him it was boring. *Man*, he thought, *I wish, just once, something exciting would happen.*

Chapter 4

The camping place for this last night on the road wasn't much. It didn't have a pool, but Andy figured, *Who would want one? All they could do was ice skate on it because it's so cold up here at night.*

One thing he liked about the cabins at the lake was the big potbellied stove in the middle of the living room. Each cabin also had a fireplace. A person could fill that stove up with logs at bedtime, and it would keep the place cozy until breakfast.

By that time, the sun was already coming up. Days around the lake were pretty warm. Andy and his sister liked to pick wild blueberries and eat them with their cereal and pancakes.

Before Andy went to bed, he tried to think how he could make his stay more exciting this year.

"Uh . . . Dad?"

"Yes?"

"Would it be okay if I only fished a little bit with you?"

"Why? Who else do you want to fish with?"

"No one."

"Well, what then?'

"Me and C J, and Jessie and Sarah want to do some exploring this time."

Sarah defiantly put her hands on her hips and huffed, "I never said. . ."

Andy broke in, "You don't have to, but we might want to look around a little more this summer . . . if that would be okay."

"We can talk about it later. I think it might be all right though."

"Thanks, Dad. You're the best."

"You always say that when you want something," his sister complained.

"Night all," Andy said.

Since it had been another long day on the road, the family went right to sleep and didn't wake up again until mid-morning. Even Andy's mother forgot to set an alarm. Andy's dad had to wake her up. "Cindy, did you forget something?"

She opened one eye and then shut it again. "Yes, I forgot I know who any of you people are."

"MOM!" Sarah gasped.

"Mother's only kidding. It just felt so good to sleep. I'll get breakfast started in a few minutes. I'm going to need some help, so stay close this morning, kids."

After breakfast, they were soon driving on the

little two-lane road again and didn't see many other cars or trucks at all.

"Did you see that?" C J called over the radio.

"See what?" Andy yelled.

"What, see what?" his father asked.

"A moose! A really big one," C J reported.

"It was a moose, Dad. No, C J, I didn't."

"Man, keep your eyes open. We could see bears and everything."

Andy looked, first on one side of the road, then the other for miles and miles. Still, he didn't see a thing. The road also changed from pavement to that gravel C J had reminded him about. It was soft under the wheels of the truck. Not only did it make a different sound, the truck occasionally slid to one side or the other. Andy's dad had to keep steering it back.

Finally, Andy heard his father say, "Almost there."

They turned onto a narrow dirt road. Branches from nearby trees scratched the sides of the truck. Some even smacked the windshield. As they passed by a sign that had "dump" painted on it, Andy couldn't believe his eyes.

"A bear . . . no wait, three of them," he screamed.

His father stopped the truck and before he could stop them, the kids jumped out to see.

That frightened the bears away. Quickly they ran among the nearby trees, then turned around to look back.

"That's why I tell you we have to keep the door to our cabin closed and the side door where we keep our trash. Those critters will come right in the house and sit at the table if you let them."

"Really?" Sarah gasped.

"Really. So be careful. Pile back in."

In only a few minutes they came to a place where their dad turned the truck to the left. Andy saw the lake, and then he noticed those familiar cabins. They weren't anything special, just cabins, but this would be home for the next two weeks.

"No phone, no TV, no nothin'," Andy sighed. "Now this is what I call *not* livin'!"

Each truck pulled in beside the two cabins where the families would be staying. Andy's dad went to the office to get the keys. When he came back, he ordered, "Time to unload everything. Then we can put our boats in the water."

There's excitement for you, Andy thought. He took his time unloading the truck. That way he figured he could put off the agony of fishing just as long as possible. After the heavy work had been done, his dad went back to the office to buy a fishing license for each member of the family.

What a waste, Andy thought. *Might as well throw the money for my license right in the lake because I don't plan to get much use out of it.* He continued helping his mother and sister with the last few bags and boxes.

Inside, the cabin was like a dark cave until Andy's mother opened all the curtains. There was a slight musty smell in the air, but once the windows were open most of that went away. The furniture hadn't exactly come up on the most recent delivery truck either. Some of the material had torn spots, and the wooden legs were nicked in several places.

The walls were still covered with knotty pine wood paneling. Andy thought the kitchen looked like something he'd seen in one of his history books. Water came out of a faucet that had to be pumped by hand. The bathroom, well, it was outside.

Andy went over and opened the two bedroom doors. "Which one is ours?" he asked, pretending not to know.

"You and Sarah get the bunk beds. Remember?"

"Top or bottom, Sarah?"

"I don't care. You pick."

"I'll take the top one then."

"Okay with me."

C J knocked on the door.

"Come in," his Aunt Cynthia called out. When she saw who it was, she added, "C J you don't have to knock. You're family."

"Thanks. Andy, you wanna look around?"

"Is it okay, Mom?"

"Sure. Just stay close for now, so we can call you."

The boys wandered down to the lake to see what was happening. Not much. One thing they did like was watching the float-planes come in and go back out.

"It must be cool to be a bush pilot in one of those things," Andy said.

"Yeah, they can take off and land on any lake they feel like. No gravel roads for them."

After a little exploring, Andy heard his mother calling. The boys scampered back to the cabins.

"We need to gather firewood for both cabins," Andy's father announced. "We'll make a work crew out of the men while the women get the cabins ready."

Firewood gathering actually took a few hours. That's because they were allowed to collect all the dead wood they could find, but it wasn't exactly near the cabins. They made several trips into the woods, came back out with a load, then went right back. After the first few trips, the dads began cutting logs into smaller pieces with their saws while the boys continued going for more wood.

On one of their trips back into the woods Andy said, "See what I mean?"

"What?" CJ asked.

"Boring, *that's* what. We gather wood, go fishing, eat, sleep, then do it all over again. It's . . . boring!"

"It's not so bad. I kinda like it up here."

"I know. So do I, but nothing ever happens here."

The wood patrol took most of the rest of the day. It was just starting to get dark when the boys' fathers returned from taking their boats to the lake. They used a cement patch that had been built right into the water so they could back the trailers in, drop the boats off, and drive back out again. Then the boats were docked at the small marina.

CJ asked his mother, "Can we take one last look at the lake before supper?"

"Yes, but come back by dark."

"We will."

Down by the water the boys saw the usual things. Boats came in with happy fishermen carrying strings of unhappy looking fish they'd caught. An occasional float-plane swooped down out of the sky, landed on the water, then powered over to a dock so more fishermen could get started the next morning. Most of the planes had just one engine in the center of the nose, and most of them looked pretty beat up from years of flying.

"I wonder how some of those junkers stay up in the air?" Andy asked.

"Or why they don't go to the bottom once they do land?" CJ added.

They turned to head back for supper when CJ said, "I like it that both our families eat supper together every night up here."

"Me, too, I . . ." Andy didn't finish his sentence. Instead, he stopped and just listened.

"What is it?" CJ asked.

"That's what I'm wondering. Don't you hear it?"

"Hear what?"

As the boys looked into the sky, neither was prepared for what was about to happen. Far off in the distance, all they could see were green and red blinking lights. But that sound! It just rumbled as it got louder. They continued watching in amazement. The lights became brighter and the sound grew louder until they were able to make out the shape of two planes, not just any planes. These were float-planes, but they weren't like any the boys had seen in all the years their families had been coming up to this lake.

"Look at them," Andy shouted barely loud enough to be heard above the approaching thunder. Then like two hungry eagles that had just spotted their dinner, the planes banked out over the water, came around in a wide circle, and lined up to land.

The airplanes were identical. Each was painted completely black. Their numbers were painted in a dark gray on the tails. These planes were big, really big. They each had two engines, not just one like all the others. Side-by-side they dropped down out of the sky, and side-by-side they touched the water at high speed.

Most of the other float-planes usually slowed down right away and came to the dock, but these planes acted like they were about to take off again, right away. They continued to skim along the water at nearly full speed.

As the boys watched, the planes disappeared behind Rocky Point which stuck far out into the water. The sound died down when they went around behind the rocks, and Andy was pretty sure he could hear the engines slowing too.

"Have you ever seen anything so great?" CJ asked.

"Never! Let's go tell our dads."

"They looked pretty scary too. Wonder what they're up to?"

"Yeah, something no good. I can tell you that."

Chapter 5

The boys ran back to the cabin where CJ's family was staying.

"Where is everybody?" he asked.

"Oh, wait a minute . . . it's our turn for supper tonight.

Yours is tomorrow."

They flew out the front, letting the screen door slam behind them. When they ran into Andy's cabin, the rest of their families were waiting.

"Where have you been? It's after dark."

"I know," Andy said. "I'm sorry, but we couldn't help it. Did you guys see those planes?"

"What planes?" the girls asked.

Andy's father crossed his arms over his chest. "You mean the black ones?"

"I sure do. We've never seen anything like them. Wait. How did you know?"

"The man who sold me our fishing licenses was telling me about them. Seems they come in every few days, always landing at night. Then, the next morning, before the sun comes up, they take off again."

"Who are they?" CJ asked.

"Nobody seems to know. Mostly they stay to themselves."

"Well, where?" Andy demanded.

"Some old private fishing lodge beyond Rocky Point. They probably just like their privacy, like me. That's all."

"But, Dad . . . two planes all painted black? They only come in at dark and leave the same way. Come on. There has to be more to it than that." Andy's mind was racing.

"There sure doesn't, and if their place is private, then that's exactly what it means. 'Leave us alone and we'll leave you alone.'"

"But, Dad. . ."

"No buts. That's final."

"I hate it when you say things like that!"

"Andrew!" his mother scolded.

"Sorry."

"Now, let's sit down and eat dinner."

Andy's mother served southern fried chicken, mashed potatoes with gravy, corn, and creamed beans.

"Where have you been hiding all this good stuff?" Andy asked.

"Weren't you the one complaining when we took time to shop back at the grocery store?" she reminded.

"That was C J, wasn't it?"

"Don't try to hook me into this one. You're on your own."

"Dad, could the girls have a spend-the-night party tonight?" Jessica asked.

"You mean stay over here with Sarah?"

"Sort of . . . I mean have her stay in my room, and C J can stay here with Andy tonight."

Andy couldn't believe what she was saying. Even if he'd tried, he couldn't have come up with a better script for what she should say. His eyes quickly darted over to C J who shrugged his shoulders and slightly shook his head as if to say, *It wasn't my idea.*

"What do the rest of the parents think?" Uncle Joe asked.

"It's fine with us, I think," Andy's mother answered.

"Then on another night, we could switch cabins and do it again," Sarah suggested.

"Let's see how it goes first, then we can decide," her mother told her.

This was just too perfect. Andy had wondered how he and his cousin were going to find the time to make plans if they were stuck in the fishing boats for the next two days. Now they could start some serious planning right away.

After dinner both families helped with the clean up.

Then they sat by the fireplace to talk.

"Did the store owner say anything more about those planes?" Andy asked.

"How long have they been coming up here?" C J added.

"He said it started a couple of weeks after the ice melted."

"Have you ever been to the old lodge?"

"No. I've seen it from the boat whenever we've fished past the point, but fishing isn't so good over there. That's why I like to go to a couple spots on the other side of the lake."

"Could we run past the lodge on our way out tomorrow. . . just to see it?"

"I'll think about it."

"What else did you find out?" Uncle Dave asked.

"The people around here are a little concerned . . . mostly because no one ever comes over from the lodge. The planes are a bit dangerous flying in and out in almost total darkness. People think a boat might get hit."

"Maybe they're just a bunch of rich people that don't wanna get too close to people like us."

"That could be. Sometimes famous people like to be left alone."

"I know," Andy laughed. "We aren't famous, but we come up here to get away from people, too."

"Well, why don't we make some plans for the

days ahead," Andy's father began. "Tomorrow evening, after a day of fishing . . ." Andy and C J looked at each other as if they were both in great pain, "dinner will be in Uncle Joe and Aunt Julie's cabin."

"What are we having?" Jessica asked.

"You'll have to wait and see."

"No fair," C J complained.

Andy's father continued, "We have to eat breakfast early so we can head to the boats by sunup."

"Wouldn't want to let those fish sleep in, would we Dad?"

"That's right. So kids, go to bed early. It'll be a short night for all of us."

"Do you plan to do anything else up here besides fish?" Andy asked.

"I sure don't."

Andy's mother asked, "Who would like some popcorn?"

Not only did the cabins have old furniture, but there were other old things like the popcorn maker hanging from the mantle. It was in the shape of a box with a long handle and a little screen door on top. Andy's mother put some oil in the bottom, and then dumped in a scoop of popcorn kernels.

"Kinda makes you miss the ol' microwave, doesn't it, Mom." Andy teased.

"Not really. When we come up here, I like to think what it must have been like for the pioneers. It makes me feel good to know I can get along without all the modern appliances I have at home."

Andy's father took the handle and placed the box over the fire. In less than a minute Andy heard a sizzling sound followed by exploding corn. Soon the smell of fresh popcorn filled the cabin making it seem a little more friendly. It took almost three batches to make enough for all eight Washburns. Then the families decided to split up for the night. Andy and CJ went to the kitchen to pump water so they could brush their teeth. After that, it was time for bed.

Andy closed the bedroom door behind them. "I think we should do like we said . . . you know . . . go fishing and then go on our own."

"What do you expect to find?" CJ asked.

"Anything but fish! That's all I need to know."

"Let's set our watches so we can get up a little early."

"What for?" Andy asked.

"Have you forgotten the planes already?"

"That's right. They leave before the sun comes up." He set his watch to go off at 4:30 AM. "I was thinking we could go out and mess around in the woods, for one thing."

"And do what?"

"I don't know. Let's just go on out and see what we can find."

"And after that?"

"What do I look like, your camp tour director? We'll just take things as they come. Who knows . . . maybe we'll find ourselves over by that old lodge or something."

"You are so sneaky."

"I know. Don't you love it?"

"What if the girls decide to get up early and come along, too?" CJ asked.

"Who cares? They're both okay to be around. I think we could all have fun."

"I guess. They usually just go off and play together anyway."

"Tell me some more about the stuff you brought with you on the trip."

"Mostly wireless technology."

"Wireless?"

"You know . . . using computers and stuff without being connected to telephone lines. The gadgets I have can be used anywhere as long as I have a generator or solar panels for power."

"Do you really think we can do that?"

"You forget who you're talking to. Give me enough time, and I'll figure out almost anything."

"That's what I like about you."

The boys talked a little longer about the fun things they could do around the lake, but it didn't take long before they were both asleep. Some time later, the most terrible sound awakened Andy. If he hadn't grabbed hold of the post, he would have fallen to the floor from his top bunk. About the same time he heard a second sound, much like the first.

"CJ, did you hear that?"

"Of course, I did. It's just our alarms doing what we told them to."

"Morning already? Ugh. I'm not ready for this."

"Be quiet. Want your parents to hear us?"

Together they sat on the bottom bunk to put on their shoes. Andy found his jacket in the corner. He slipped it on, then crept over to the door. The latch made a loud sound when he turned the knob, but that was nothing compared to the creaking made by the old metal hinges.

"We're gonna get caught for sure," C J whispered.

"Shhh. . . ."

It seemed like every board in the floor was just waiting for someone to step on it because when the boys did, each one made a different noise. Almost like, "Ouch! Hey! Get off me! Who do you think you're walking on?"

Finally, the cousins made it to the front door. It had locks on it, but up here most people didn't bother. Andy opened it easily, and they slipped out. The air was cold, even colder than at their last campsite. The sky seemed darker than usual. Andy looked up and noticed there were no stars and the moon was missing. Then he felt the most wonderful thing of all.

"Was that a raindrop?" he asked.

"I think I felt one, too." Rain continued to fall as Andy began jumping up and down. "It's raining. It's raining!"

"Do you have to be so loud?"

"Don't you know what this means?"

"Yeah. It means it's raining."

"And when it rains, we can't go . . ."

"FISHING!"

A feeling of excitement rushed through Andy as the two boys started jumping around. They would have kept on jumping except for what they heard. It was that sound like the same one from the night before.

"Let's run to the lake," CJ called. When they got there, the boys could hardly breathe, and when they did, their breath made it look like they were standing outside back home in January.

Andy and CJ turned to look in the direction of Rocky Point just in time to see the two mysterious sets of lights moving slowly in the water. The low rumble became a loud roar as both planes went to full power. Slowly, they began to pick up speed, skimming along the water like champion skiers. If it hadn't been for their lights, the boys would have only heard the noise and seen nothing. In just minutes the mysterious planes appeared to lift off from the surface of the water and bank into the dark morning sky. Then they were gone.

We gotta get over to that place and find out what's going on, Andy thought.

Chapter 6

The rain was falling steadily as Andy hit the front door of his cabin.

"Hi, Mom, what's for breakfast?"

"Are you up already? I thought you weren't very interested in fishing this year."

"Me and CJ got up early so we could watch the planes take off."

"Which planes were those?"

"From the lodge . . . you know . . . the two black ones."

"I thought I heard something. It woke me up."

"They really are something to see, Mom."

"Oh, no, is that rain I hear?"

Andy brushed water from his jacket. "No, Mom. Did you think I fell in the lake?" he teased.

"Your father isn't going to like the rain."

"Yeah, isn't it great?"

"I'll let him sleep in this morning. It's such a long trip up here."

"Hey, seven-thirty," Andy's father said as he

stumbled out of his bedroom. "How come you didn't wake me?"

"I did try."

"It's raining out, Dad."

"Really? Some of the best fishing is in the rain."

"We still have to . . . I mean, get to go out today?"

"Sure, why not? I just don't like being on the lake when there's lightening or a strong wind."

"Oh."

"I think the girls can stay in, but us men . . . we have a job to do if people expect to eat any fish while we're up here." He and Andy ate their breakfast, and as they finished, it looked like CJ had gotten the same bad news. He was already wearing his rain jacket and rain pants. The look on his face said, *Uh huh, and don't ask me about it.*

Andy and his father gathered their fishing gear from the back room along with their waterproof clothes. "Why don't we just take out one boat this morning," Uncle Joe suggested, "since there'll only be four of us."

"Good idea."

The four adventurers began walking toward the docks.

Andy wondered if this was what it felt like for men back in history who were expected to hunt and fish for the food their families needed. That thought made going out on the water this morning a little easier to take. Having CJ in the same boat would make it more fun, too.

Gentle rain fell from the light gray sky. The lake was calm. As they began heading out, a single engine float plane made its final approach and lightly touched down on the water. *No wonder those guys like to fly so early*, Andy thought. It would be like racing over railroad tracks if they waited till the middle of the day because by that time the lake is usually pretty choppy.

His dad's fishing spot was over an hour across the lake. He kept maps, depth meters, and water temperature gauges in his boat along with just about every gadget a fisherman could want. It reminded Andy of all the computer junk CJ got to play with.

"Where are we headed today?" Andy asked.

"There's a rocky island I want to try this morning. We just need to catch enough for a couple of dinners."

"What are we looking for?"

"Walleyes mostly."

"How do we find those?"

"They hang around the rocks over here, but so do Northern Pike. They like to ambush the Walleyes in this spot."

"Ambush?"

"They hunt them for food."

"You mean fish eat each other?"

"They certainly do."

"I'm sure glad people aren't like that."

"There are some. You've heard about cannibals haven't you?"

"I didn't think that happened anymore."

"You know what the one cannibal said to the other cannibal, don't you?"

"No, what?"

"Come over to my hut tonight, I'd like to have you for dinner."

"No, really, Dad. Are there still people like that?"

"Yes, in some remote areas. In this world, not every one plays by the same rules. You take those poachers for instance."

"What poachers?"

"The ones we saw at the border. They were trying to break the law just to make money, and they got caught at it. Now, they have to pay the price. Not playing by the rules is never worth it." He continued driving his boat a little longer, then announced, "There it is."

Up ahead, huge boulders stuck part way out of the water. The island where they were going looked like it was made from nothing but rocks. The boat slowed and came to a stop. Andy's father dropped an anchor into the water and let out the rope till the anchor hit bottom. Then he tied the other end to his boat.

"Remember, boys," Uncle Joe told them, "the Pike is the easiest fish to catch up here. So, today we want to keep only the biggest ones. The others we'll just catch and release."

"Why would we want to let any of them go?" CJ asked.

"So they can keep growing for us to catch another time when we come up. Besides, there's still a lot of commercial fishing on this lake."

"You mean with the nets we've seen?" Andy asked.

"It's been happening less over the years, but a lot of fish are still taken out of the lake that way. It's the Walleye we're mostly after today."

After about an hour of fishing, the rain let up, and in another, it quit completely. After that, the sun began to peek out from behind the clouds. Andy and the others took off their rain gear. Andy's father handed him a couple towels to wipe water from the seats.

It wouldn't be exactly fair to call what the Washburns did over the next several hours fishing. They may have been fishing for Walleyes, but a lot of Northern Pike were in the same waters. One thing for sure about Northerns, they are an extremely aggressive fish. That meant that no matter who threw what into the water a

Northern Pike was likely to strike at the end of the line. And strike they did! Occasionally, someone in the boat managed to pull in a Walleye which was always followed by great celebration.

The day actually went by quickly which surprised Andy.

He was expecting to hate being out on the water, but he caught a lot of fish. Most of them had to be thrown back because they were too small, but he'd had fun. Among the group of four fishermen, they caught a total of six Walleye, along with enough large Northerns to make a good dinner. Each managed to catch his daily limit.

"Time to head back?" Uncle Joe asked.

"You're right. I wasn't paying much attention. Would you pull up the anchor? I'll start the motor."

Andy liked that sound. It meant they'd soon be back in their warm cabins. He was looking forward to finding out what Aunt Julie was cooking since she wouldn't tell him.

"It'll be getting dark soon. We should have left earlier," Andy's father said. He moved the selector as far forward as it would go. At first the nose of the boat stuck straight up in the air while the back sank down low in the water. It didn't take long until their boat leveled off. When it did that, they sliced through the waves at high speed.

The boat wasn't one of those wimpy little bass boats. This one had a car engine right about in the middle of the boat, driving the propeller in the back. The powerful engine had a cover over it, but the noise was still pretty loud. Andy's dad told him they could easily water ski behind it except that the water was way too cold for that. A two-way radio was kept on the boat for safety. Andy's mother had a base unit in their cabin and so did Aunt Julie.

Just then Andy heard, "Base to Stinky Fisherman. Where are you guys?"

"Sorry. We stayed a little late out here. We're on our way back now. Should make it just around dark."

"Okay, be careful out there."

"We will."

Their boat continued to race toward the other side of the lake. Dore Lake was so big, once a boat was out in the middle, there was nothing to see in all directions except water. It felt like the ocean or one of the Great Lakes. The water got pretty rough at times, too. Where Andy's boat was, the waves made the boat go up high, then slam back down into the water. Andy liked to stand up, hold on to the rail, and pretend he was riding a wild bucking horse. Standing also helped him not to get seasick.

As they came closer to their cabins, the water became calmer. Andy wondered if that's why people built cabins on this side of the lake in the first place. It would be tough to park some of the float-planes at the docks if the waves were high all the time. Taking off or landing would be even tougher.

That's when he heard it. It was the unmistakable sound of the twin monsters he and CJ had seen taking off.

Couldn't be them, Andy thought. *They're only suppose to come in every week or so.* He searched the horizon for the familiar lights. "CJ, do you hear them?"

His cousin was sitting at the back of the boat where the dual exhaust pipes rumbled like a drag racer. "Hear what?" he shouted back.

"Come up here where I am."

CJ pulled himself along the rail. As he got there, the two black planes went right over their heads.

"Those idiots!" Andy's father shouted. "They're going to kill someone."

The planes banked out over the lake, just like the night before, then slowly dropped out of the sky. They were heading right for the Washburn boat. When they flew overhead, Andy was sure he could reach up and touch one of the pontoons.

As they passed, everyone in the boat felt the heat from their powerful engines. The sound was so loud they had to cover their ears.

"They didn't miss us by much," Andy's father shouted in alarm.

"We should report them," CJ suggested.

The planes hit the water at full speed and continued on around Rocky Point.

"Hey, Dad, you said we could look at the lodge this morning."

"It was raining, and I forgot. Sorry."

"Well, it's too dark now, isn't it?"

"I think so, and we're late. It's partly our fault for being on the water when it is so dark. It's dangerous."

The boat eased up to its spot at the dock. Andy jumped out with one of the ropes and tied it tight. CJ went off the back and did the same.

"Let's make sure to get everything in one trip. It's too dark to come back later."

That meant they had to put all their rain clothes back on because it would be impossible to carry all the fishing equipment, the heavy fish they'd caught, and the rain gear too. They couldn't carry one more thing as they walked from the dock toward the warm light coming from the cabins. The air had already turned cold like it did every night.

"Hey, Dave," Uncle Joe said. "I thought the store manager told you the planes don't come up here that often."

"He did. Must be somebody real important."

Real important my foot, Andy thought. Seeing those planes two days in a row convinced him that the people over at the old lodge were up to no good. One more day of family fishing fun, and he was determined to find out what it was.

Chapter 7

As he hit the front door, Andy was sure he smelled roast beef. Aunt Julie was almost as good a cook as his mom. He noticed cornbread, a vegetable casserole, and two of the most beautiful, fresh, wild blueberry pies in the whole world.

"Let's eat," Andy ordered.

"This isn't our house," his mother reminded him. Conversation around the table included talk about how the fishing went. The girls had played house almost all day because the rain lasted longer around the cabins than where the boat had been. The mothers enjoyed reading and resting.

"Did we hear those planes again tonight?" Aunt Julie asked.

"We weren't going to say anything, but they nearly hit us on our way in."

"Hit you? Really?"

"We shouldn't have been out in the dark. I won't let that happen again."

The girls had also moved everything back

after their spend-the-night party which meant that Andy and CJ wouldn't be able to make their plans as easily. They also knew they'd be out fishing in the morning anyway.

After dinner, the families sat around the fire again, and the grown-ups told family stories. This was a time to catch up on a little history. Some of the stories were pretty funny, but since Andy didn't know most of the people they were telling about, it wasn't all that interesting to him. His mind wandered to thoughts of how he intended to spend the rest of his vacation.

When it came time to split up for the night, he caught CJ by the arm. "Tomorrow we fish again like we agreed. But after that, let's plan to do some exploring. Deal?"

"Deal."

But it was raining the next morning.

Not again, Andy thought. He looked at his watch. It was almost eight o'clock. *That doesn't seem right*, he thought. He dropped down quietly out of the top bunk to the floor because his sister was still a long way from waking up. In the kitchen he found his parents sitting at the table.

"It's late, Dad. When we going out?"

"I think we'll give it a rest. With all the fish we brought in yesterday, they should hold us for a couple meals anyway."

Besides, the excitement that always comes from the first day of fishing had come and gone.

"But I thought . . ." Andy didn't finish his sentence. He didn't want to give away the fact that he had no plans to go fishing again after today. "Can I mess around with CJ then?"

"Sure, if his parents don't have plans."

"I'll go check."

"You need to eat your breakfast first," his mother reminded. "It's the most important meal of the day."

Andy quickly ate two pieces of toast and drank a glass of juice. "Now, is it okay?"

"Go ahead."

He grabbed a rain jacket, put it over his head, and ran to the other cabin. CJ and his sister were already working a large puzzle.

"What's the picture going to be?" Andy asked.

"My parents wanted to make sure it kept us busy for days."

"How would they know?"

"Well, just look at the box."

Andy picked it up from an empty chair next to the table. "Which is up and which is down?"

"Does it really matter?" Jessica asked.

"Well, yeah."

CJ took a deep breath. "I figure it's either a picture that's half clouds and half blue sky or half water and half clouds."

"Either way it looks impossible," Andy observed.

"I think that's the idea."

"You want to come over later?" Andy asked. "We can go to my room and work with your computer."

"Sure, this should only take another year or so. Then I'll come."

"Seriously, how soon can you be over?"

"I'll bring my stuff in about fifteen minutes."

"Okay, I can clear a place."

"My dad will let me use the generator. We can run my laptop all day if we want to."

"Great, see you in a few." Andy went back to his cabin and into his room. He was happy to see that Sarah had gotten up already. He made some room on the table and cleared two of the chairs.

A few minutes later CJ came bounding through the door with the laptop under his arm. "Ready to go to work?"

"Work? What do you mean?"

"I thought since we didn't have to go out today, we could look up information about poaching."

"And see if it's a big problem?" Andy asked.

"That's what I was thinking. Hang on a minute. I have to drag the generator around and pass you a plug through your window." He dashed out of the room and quickly appeared outside.

Andy had already opened his window a crack.

"Here. Take this end and plug in the power strip."

As soon as Andy did that, CJ returned to his room.

"Where do you get all this computer stuff?" Andy asked.

"All kinds of companies want my dad to carry their products. I get to test some of it for him and say what I think. This system is made up from different suppliers. I can contact the satellite with this black box here."

"How does that work?"

"You know when you're watching the news and there's a report from some part of the world that's in the middle of nowhere?"

"Yeah, I always wondered how they did that."

"Satellites. The world is surrounded with them. We just dial one in with the dish out there, send our signal, and we're in. It's as easy as that."

"Easy for you. Are we ready yet?"

"Sure, let's get started."

For the next hour the boys hooked an uplink dish and a downlink dish to a controller. That box was connected to the black box CJ needed to encode and decode the information. Then CJ ran back outside and fired up his dad's generator for power to run the system. Once everything was set, the boys were ready.

CJ punched up his favorite search engine and entered the word 'poachers'. In only seconds, the first page of entries popped up.

He pointed to the screen. "Look at that . . . seventy-three thousand places to check."

"Try *poaching*," Andy suggested.

"Wow! This says there're a hundred and sixteen thousand."

"No way! We don't have that much time. Scroll down and we can pick out a few to look at." Over the next hour the boys read that poaching was a worldwide problem.

Andy pointed to the screen. "Check that one."

When CJ clicked on it, he began to read out loud, *"Last summer, state and federal agents, armed with a search warrant, went into the house where they found dozens of reptiles and amphibians. Included in the pens were endangered species. In another room they found rattlesnakes and alligators."*

Andy studied the screen. "Man, that's just like the people we saw at the border."

"Wonder if they were part of this bunch?" CJ asked.

At another site, CJ read what one FBI agent said. *"Cases can take months, even years to solve. Poachers know their business. Wildlife shipments generate six billion* dollars each year. It's second only to drugs in profitability. So, it isn't difficult to see why people get into it."

"Six billion!" Andy exclaimed. "What else does it say?"

"Says here, '*A new report reveals that organized criminal gangs, including the Russian Mafia and South American drug cartels, are using existing smuggling routes for illegal items such as small arms and drugs to trade in the highly profitable wildlife.*'"

"And check this out," CJ continued. "*Fifty percent of wildlife criminals have previous convictions for drugs, violence, theft and firearms offenses.*"

"These are some dangerous people, aren't they?"

"Very. Look. Here's a story from around here."

"At Dore?"

"No, . . . Canada. It says people could order a tiger on the Internet. Then they'd have it shipped to a place that doesn't have any regulations about exotic animals or where the police aren't very strong."

"Well, that sounds exactly like the kind of place where we are right now."

"Look," CJ continued. "Here's the same thing the border guard told your dad. In Europe, they'll pay between $20,000 and $50,000 for an Indian headdress if it has golden or bald eagle feathers.

Somebody up in Alaska caught a gyrfalcon and sold it to a guy in Saudi Arabia for $100,000."

"What's a gyrfalcon?"

"I don't know. I'll look it up." CJ typed the name into his browser. When the sites came up, he tried one. "Oh, look, it's just another kind of falcon. You know . . . those birds that catch other birds and eat them."

"A bird of prey, that's right." Andy said.

"I know. I used to have the worst time figuring out the difference between p-r-e-y, like this bird would eat, and p-r-a-y, like we do before we eat."

"So, is there anything we can do about poachers if we find them?"

"This anti-poaching group says you should contact their website. It's a place where people can report poachers."

"Let's save it for later."

"Good idea."

"You wanna play some video games for awhile?"

"Yes, but no fishing games, okay?" Andy laughed. They went into the kitchen to make sandwiches for lunch. Andy liked the way things were more relaxed up North. There were fewer rules to worry about than he was used to back home. After lunch, they continued playing in Andy's room.

Dinner was also at Andy's cabin tonight. He

hadn't paid much attention to the activities outside his room until he and CJ thought they smelled fish frying. They hurried to the kitchen to see. "What're we having?"

"Fish, followed by fish, and topped off with more fish," his mother told him. "Plus, cornbread and lots of other things you don't like."

"Funny, Mom. I like everything I see and smell," he smiled.

After dinner, the families again gathered around the fireplace. "So," Andy's dad began, "let's talk about tomorrow."

"What about it?" Andy asked.

"The weather forecast is for clear and warmer. Since we ate most of what we caught already, we need to re-stock our fish pile."

"Well, CJ and I had an idea."

"What is that?"

"We wondered if the Moms want to go out."

"There are two boats you know," Uncle Joe reminded him.

"I know, but the four of you could spend time on the water together."

"And what would you boys be doing?"

"Yeah, . . . and us girls too?" Sarah asked.

"I don't know about the two of you, but we'd like to go explore and play in the woods," Andy continued.

"Me, too," Jessica added.

"Would that work for you boys?" Andy's dad asked.

"Sure, it's okay with us."

"Do you think the children would be safe . . . alone?" Andy's mother asked.

"We'll be fine, Mom," Andy assured her.

"Then that settles it. The grown-ups will go fishing and the four of you can take the day off."

"Great. Thanks," Andy said. Later he told CJ, "At least we got part of what we wanted."

"Yeah, but the girls will really tie us down."

"They should be okay. Remember, we can check out that old lodge."

"The lodge! Man, I almost forgot about it."

Chapter 8

When morning came, Andy didn't need anyone to wake him up. He was excited about getting out into the woods and not having to spend another day on the water. CJ must have felt the same way because he came bounding into the room.

"Come on you sleeping slug, the day is getting away from us. Get up, Sarah. My sister is dressed and had her breakfast already."

"Wait for us in the kitchen. We'll be right out," Andy suggested.

After breakfast, the children helped their parents carry some of the things they'd need for fishing down to the boat.

"Now, you kids be careful," Aunt Julie warned.

"We will," CJ answered. "And you kids be careful on the lake, too," he teased. After the boat was out of sight, the children headed out toward the dense woods. Once they had walked into the forest for a few minutes, Andy stopped. "You guys notice how quiet it is in here? I can't hear planes, boats, or anything."

"We have to be careful not to get lost. There aren't a lot of signs," CJ joked.

"Plus, I remember you have a horrible sense of direction," Andy noted. "Good thing I was born with a compass in my head. Let's go over this way. I want to find out if we can see the lodge."

"Mom told us to be careful," Jessica reminded them.

"It won't hurt to look," Andy told her.

The massive trees didn't allow for the sun to shine down to the ground. Because of that, there wasn't much brush to slow them down. The ground was covered with rotten branches and leaves that looked as if they'd been there for years. They felt soft and thick under Andy's feet like an expensive carpet.

"Over this way," he pointed. The rest of the children followed until they all came to a stop in front of a high fence.

"What is a huge fence like that doing in the middle of the woods?" CJ demanded.

Andy looked up to the top. "It has all that barbed wire up there. I don't think it's possible to get over the thing."

"Climb it? Are you crazy?" Jessica asked.

"We want to see what those people are up to at the lodge."

"Sarah and I don't."

"Well, you don't have much choice either. You have to stay with us."

"Then let's do something more fun than stare at a dumb fence."

"Okay. You got any ideas?"

"I do," CJ interrupted.

Andy gave him a look that said, *I thought you were on my side*, but his cousin ignored it. "We could build a fort like they had in the frontier days."

"That sounds like fun," Sarah added. "We could pretend like we're the first people to move here, and we need a place to keep the animals away."

"Is that anything like playing house?" Andy asked. "You know how much I hate playing house."

"No, it's a fort," his sister assured him.

"Then let's get building."

The children ran back to an area of the woods they had passed where over a hundred small trees had died. "What happened to all these trees?" CJ asked.

Andy looked at them scattered over the ground. They looked like toothpicks a giant had used, then thrown away. The thought of a giant gave him a shiver.

"There isn't any sunlight in here. They probably died because of that."

"Sure," Jessica said. "Last year my mom moved

some plants in from the patio for the winter. She put a few of them in a room that didn't get much sun. Those plants died in only a couple weeks, but the ones she put by windows and by the sliding glass door did great."

"Who cares why they died? They're dead. Now, let's use them for our fort," CJ ordered.

"We have to go back to the cabins and get a hatchet, one of our dad's saws, and some rope. We need a bunch of stuff," Andy announced.

CJ and the girls ran to see what they could find. Andy didn't move. When the others realized he wasn't with them, they stopped and looked back to see him standing right where they had left him.

"Come on," CJ called. "Aren't you going to help us?"

"Sure I am, but if you keep running in that direction, the next time anybody sees you, you'll be in North Dakota."

"North Dakota?" Jessica asked as they came back.

"The cabins aren't in that direction, are they?" CJ asked.

"Nowhere near. Now if you will all just follow me. . . ." Then Andy led them in a different direction. Soon, they walked back into the camp where their cabins were. It only took a few minutes to gather the things they needed, and the four were back on their way into the woods. For the rest of the day, the boys spent most of their time cutting logs into the same lengths. The girls made brooms out of dead branches and began clearing an area where the fort would go.

No one noticed it was beginning to get dark because all day long it never was very light under the big trees. So, when the dark did come, it came fast.

"Andy, shouldn't we start back?" Sarah asked.

Andy took one look at his watch and ordered, "Quick, put all the tools and stuff in a pile. We can cover them with sticks and come back tomorrow to work on this place again."

By the time they did that, it was very dark. Now it was really important that Andy had a good sense of direction. *I wonder where they would wind up if they can't find their way out of this place in the daytime?* he thought.

After the final sticks and leaves were placed on the pile, they turned to leave. That's when Andy saw it. "Guys," he said in a trembling voice. "Look!"

The cousins peered through the forest as strange lights danced across their faces. "Get down," CJ ordered.

They just managed to drop to the ground before six all-terrain vehicles came storming right past where they were hiding and quickly disappeared deeper into the woods.

"What was that?" Jessica asked.

"Not what. Who!" Andy responded. "Let's get out of here." The children ran for a few minutes, then turned to see if they were safe. In the distance they could still see the faint glimmer of those lights.

When they arrived back at the cabins, their parents were already there. Waiting!

"Where have you kids been?" Uncle Joe asked.

"We were playing in the woods," CJ told him. "All day it's dark back there. We lost track of time. Then it got really dark all of a sudden."

"Tell them about the . . . ." CJ clamped his hand over his sister's mouth. She didn't like that, so she bit his finger. "Ouch! What did you do that for?"

"Tell us about what?"

"Never mind," all four children said together.

Dinner tonight was at CJ's cabin. "How was the fishing today?" he asked.

"We didn't do as well as when you boys went with us. We talked a lot more, and I think that may have scared the fish."

"Maybe, but the moms enjoyed the day, that's

for sure," Andy's mother told them.

"So, what was it you wanted to tell us about?" Uncle Joe asked.

"Lights. We saw some strange lights in the woods," Jessica said. The other three children gave her an angry stare.

"What kind of lights?"

"They were strange. I mean, they danced all over the place at first."

"I know," Andy's father said. "We saw them too."

"You did?" all four cousins gasped.

"Sure, that happens up here every year, don't you remember?"

Now, Andy, his sister, and their cousins didn't know what to think. "Exactly what did your lights look like?" Andy asked.

"You know, dancing lights," Aunt Julie said. "Red, yellow, green, blue, violet, pink . . . they were beautiful."

Sarah began, "Our lights were . . . " but she quit when her brother kicked her ankle under the table.

"Ow, that hurt."

"What hurt?" her mother asked.

"Oh, nothing."

"What's going on with you children tonight?" their father asked. "You're all so secretive."

"Nothing, Dad. Tell us more about *your* lights."

"You remember. It's the *Aurora borealis*. The Northern Lights."

"That's right. We saw them from the dock last year. Remember, I brought home that paper from school telling us all about how they work."

"How do they work?" Jessica asked.

"It's a little complicated," Uncle Joe began. "The easiest way to tell you is that there are all of these little particles in the air. Each one has an electrical charge. They run into other particles in our atmosphere that have gas in them. That's when the fireworks begin."

"Where does the electricity come from?"

"That's from the sun. The colors come from the different kinds of gas particles that crash into each other."

"But we never see them at home. How come?" CJ asked.

"They do come down that far into the country sometimes, but one of the best places to see them is right here where we are now. It gets better around November since it's so dark then. The other thing is that they are at their brightest and best every eleven years. We just happen to be up here at a good time to see them."

"There are many ancient legends about the lights," Andy's father added.

"Do you know any of them?" Andy asked.

"Years ago, people in Alaska thought they were spirits of the animals they'd hunted. Others around the world believed they were the lights from torches or campfires."

By this time, the parents had completely forgotten about the *other* lights. Dinner was soon finished, and it was fireplace time again. Andy looked forward to fireplace time every night. It was a time when he felt especially close to his family. Having his aunt, uncle, and cousins there, made him feel that the world was safe for now.

Andy's father stared into the fire for a long time. "When we come up here, I'm reminded of what life must have been like in the world before electricity, big cities, and the fast pace we live in today. I like to remember that Jesus' disciples were mostly fishermen. One of my favorite stories in the Bible is where Jesus told his followers to go out and tell other people about Him. He encouraged them to become fishers of men. I really like that part. Who can think of other stories about fish in the Bible?"

"I like the time when He fed the five thousand with just a few fish and a little bread. Man, I would love to have been there to see that," CJ said.

Jessica thought for a moment. "My favorite is the one when the men fished all night and didn't catch anything at all. Then Jesus told them to put the nets on the other side of the boat. I think it made them a little mad at first, but then they did it."

"Yeah, and when they did what He told them to, they almost caught more fish than they could pull in," Andy added.

"Does anyone have a joke about fishing?" Andy's father asked. No one came up with one. Then Uncle Joe said, "It's not a joke, but I saw an interesting short movie on TV about the reverse of fishing."

"The reverse? What is that?" Andy asked.

"Yeah, tell us," others begged.

"Let me see. There was this guy walking along the side of a lake just minding his own business. What do you think happened?"

"What?" Jessica asked.

"An apple came sailing up out of the water heading toward the beach. Plop! It landed in the soft sand right in front of the man. Well first he looked at the apple, then he looked all around to see where it had come from. He was very hungry."

"Where did it come from?" Sarah asked.

"He didn't know, but when he leaned down to pick it up, the apple jumped away about two feet. So he moved toward it again, but when he did, it jumped another two feet away. This happened a few more times until the man had had all he could take."

"Then what did he do?" CJ asked.

"He watched it for a couple more seconds. Then like a diving champion he sprang out and fell on the apple. With one hand he grabbed it. Then the man stood up, polished the apple on his sweater, raised it to his mouth. . ."

"Don't eat it! Tell him not to eat it, Daddy," Jessica cried.

"He took the biggest bite out of that apple. It was red. It was juicy. And it was the sweetest apple the man had ever tasted. Then, without warning, his head snapped to one side so he was looking out onto the lake. There was a yank, then a harder pull. The man fought hard, but he was pulled first into the shallow water, then out where it was deep. Finally, there were just a few bubbles as his hat floated away."

"Is that the end?" Andy asked. "If it is, that's the worst story I've ever heard. No wonder I don't care much about fishing."

"It's not the end."

"It isn't?" Sarah and Jessica shrieked. Sarah grabbed her mother's arm and held on tight.

"No sooner did the hat float away than another apple came sailing out of the water. Plop! It landed in the soft sand on the beach."

Sarah gripped onto her mother's arm harder

than before.

"I'm never going to eat another apple as long as I live," she declared.

"That's a good story, Joe," Andy's father said. "You had me going. Thanks. Before we break up for the night, let's sing that little song, *I will Make You Fishers of Men.*'"

"Sort of takes on a whole new meaning, doesn't it?" Uncle Joe chuckled.

The families sang together, forming a small choir. That sound, mixed with the soft glow from the fire gave Andy goose bumps.

"Who's going out in the boat tomorrow?" Uncle Joe asked.

"Julie and I are planning to do some serious baking," Andy's mother told them.

"Us kids want to go back in the woods. We're building a fort back there," Andy added.

"Is that where some of my tools went?" his father asked.

"Yes, but they're safe."

"Well, Joe. Looks like it's just you and me, bud."

"Sounds fine to me. Look out you fish!" he announced.

"Promise you won't eat any apples out there," Andy's mother joked.

"We won't."

That night, Andy went to bed thinking about the design for the fort they would start building in the morning. He also remembered the men he'd seen in the woods. That, added to the information about poachers he and his cousin found earlier on the Internet, worried him.

Chapter 9

After breakfast the next day, everyone split up for the activities they had chosen: fishing, baking, and fort building. The children headed for the woods with lunches their mothers had packed for them. When they came to the place of the dead trees, Andy was relieved to see their tools were right where he had hidden them. "First, we have to make a frame," he ordered.

Andy pulled a piece of paper out of his back pocket. "Here, I made a drawing last night before I went to bed."

"Will it be like a house?" Sarah asked.

"I told you about playing house. It's a fort, with high walls, lookout posts, and a gate to come in and out. It is not going to be anything like a house."

For the rest of the morning, the children followed Andy's plans. By lunchtime, the four main support poles were up and two of the crosspieces.

"It's taking shape real nice," CJ noted. "Where did you come up with the plans?"

"From my head. I can see pictures of things like this in my head. From there I just draw it up."

"Wish I could do that," CJ sighed.

"Yeah, but you're great with computers. We all have different things to be good at."

"I guess so."

As they ate lunch, the children noticed how quiet the woods seemed. No sound could get through the thick growth of trees. After they finished eating, Andy wasn't sure if he wanted to take a nap or keep working. "I'm wiped out. What do you think about quitting for now, so we can do some more exploring?"

"This fort isn't going anywhere," CJ said. "What do you girls think?"

"Exploring sounds fun to me," Jessica said.

Again they put their tools under the sticks and leaves as before. When Andy was sure they were safely hidden, he led the others off toward another part of the woods. Soon, they found a path that had been worn into the ground from years of someone or something walking on it.

But who . . . what . . . and where were they going? Andy wondered. He decided to follow the trail and see where it went. The path wasn't straight. Instead, it wound around in the trees, first uphill, then down again. After about thirty minutes, CJ asked. "Andy. Do you think we should turn back? We promised not to stay out past dark this time."

"The path looks like it goes straight up that hill. Let's see if there's anything up there. If not, we can start back."

By the time they reached the top of the steep hill, everyone was out of breath. The children flopped down in a grassy meadow to rest, but Andy noticed something right away. "Look over there," he shouted as he pointed off in the distance.

"What is that?" Sarah asked.

"I'm not sure, but I think it's a fire tower."

"What are they for?"

"Nobody uses them as much as they used to. When they were first built, men had the job of sitting in them all day to watch for fires. I guess they might still get used if it's real dry."

"Let's go see it," CJ suggested.

Off they ran toward the tower with new energy and excitement. Andy got there first. He looked straight up and that made his neck hurt. "I'll bet we could see forever from up there."

"Then let's go," CJ added.

Slowly and carefully the children climbed the metal ladder. At the top, they came to an opening that led to a walkway around the outside of the tower. A railing kept them from falling off. Andy peered in a window. The inside looked like a small apartment.

"Did people live up here?" Jessica asked.

"Sometimes they had to stay for a long time," Andy told them.

"Hey, isn't that our lake over there?"

"I think it is," Andy answered. "And that looks like Rocky Point."

"Where?" CJ asked.

Andy pointed. "Over there, see?"

"I think so. Then that must be the lodge farther to the left."

"You're right. It is. From up here we could spy on those guys."

"Come on. Now I'm getting scared," Jessica whimpered.

"They can't get us way up here. You don't need to worry," CJ comforted.

Andy got an idea. "We can get my dad's telescope. You know, the one he brings up to look at stars?"

"Sure. With that thing we can almost climb right inside the lodge with those creeps," CJ suggested.

"That's it, then. We'll go back to our cabins for tonight. Then in the morning, we can come straight up here after our fishing fathers hit the lake."

They returned to the cabins. The children all went into Andy's cabin and found the sweet smell of a bakery.

"Yum!" Andy exclaimed. He could hardly

believe all the cookies. There were brownies, biscuits, muffins, two pies, and a cake spread out on the table and counter top. "Who are you planning to feed all this stuff to?" he asked.

"Well," his mother began. "There are eight of us. If you just do a little math, and divide what you see by eight, if we're really hungry, you'll find it shouldn't take very long till we'll need to do this again."

Andy smacked his lips. "I'll be happy to do my part to make that day come as soon as possible."

Since the mothers had worked hard baking everything, they decided to make supper a little simpler. Along with the other baking, they'd made several loaves of bread. These were already sliced ready for the families to build their own sandwiches. Just then both fathers came in from the boat. "What smells so good?" Uncle Joe asked.

"It isn't us," CJ laughed.

His father smiled. "I'd never make that mistake, son."

After everyone had begun eating, Andy's father said, "I can see what the moms have been doing all day, and our ice chests prove what Uncle Joe and I did, but what have you all been up to?"

"Well, we worked on our fort most of the day."

"Yeah, then we found this really great . . . Ow!"

"What made you say that, Sarah?" her

mother asked.

"Oh, it's nothing."

"How many fish did you catch?" Andy asked.

"Got our limit again. It's hard not to catch those Northern."

Later that night, after the families had gone to bed, Andy slipped out of his room to get the telescope his dad kept in the front closet. He brought it back to his room and slid it under Sarah's bed. When he got up the next morning, his Father and Uncle Joe were already gone.

Perfect, Andy thought.

After a quick breakfast and after Andy had slipped the telescope out his window, the children were off on their fire tower adventure. They ran as fast as they could until the path again came to the steep hill.

"Let's walk it from here," Andy said. "My side is killing me."

When they reached the meadow, all four cousins raced again to see who could get to the tower first. Since Andy was carrying the telescope, even the girls beat him. By the time he got to the ladder, the others were already halfway up. It was more difficult for him to climb with the bulky telescope. Twice he almost dropped it. *Dad would kill me if I smashed this thing*, he thought fearfully. Finally, he made it safely to the top.

"Here, take this," he begged as he pushed the case through the opening.

For the next hour, they enjoyed taking turns looking at boats on the water, birds, and people far away on the docks. Occasionally, Andy turned his attention toward the old lodge. "Man, the lodge is a mess," he informed the others. "I don't see how they could be bringing important people up to that dump."

"Here, let me see," CJ said. He, too, looked around the lodge. "That place is awful. Who would want to stay there?"

"I don't know," Andy replied as he took the telescope back.

He began to study the area more closely. Clearly there were men walking in and out of the building. He could make out other smaller sheds and buildings near the main lodge. The men he saw moved in and out of those places too. He let CJ and the girls take turns, but none of them saw anything more than he had told them about already.

When CJ took his turn again, he whispered, "Andy, come here. You gotta see this."

"See what?"

"There are eight guys down there moving two cages, and each cage has a full grown tiger in it."

"Let us see," Sarah cried.

"Give me that!" Andy demanded as he pulled the telescope away from his cousin. He looked through the eyepiece, but as he brought the picture into clearer focus he saw something else that scared him so bad, he couldn't speak. He was looking directly into the face of another man who was staring right back at him through high-powered binoculars.

Andy jumped back against the tower, and when he did, he pushed himself away from the telescope. Almost as if in slow motion, it went over the side, tripod and all.

"What did you do that for?" CJ shouted.

"You're really gonna get it from Dad," Sarah warned.

Andy could feel his face turn completely white. "I gotta sit down," he barely whispered as he slumped to the floor.

"What's wrong? What did you see?" Jessica cried.

"Andy, you don't look so good," CJ warned.

Andy managed to swallow. Then he took his first breath since slamming against the tower. In a forced whisper he said, "We gotta get off this thing as fast as we can."

"But why?"

"Don't ask me now. Down first! Then I can talk about it."

They were just about to start down the ladder when something even worse happened. The two black floatplanes flew directly over the tower. They were so close, the cousins actually saw the people in both airplanes glaring directly at them.

"This is serious," Andy gasped.

"I'm scared," Sarah cried.

"Down, let's just get down. Now!"

As soon as they reached the bottom of the tower, Andy gathered up what used to be his father's valuable telescope. Then he and the cousins ran for the trees. At least in there, Andy thought, they might be safe. When they came back to the fort they had been building, he signaled for the others to stop.

"All right. Now, tell us what you saw," CJ demanded.

Completely out of breath he began, "I . . . I . . . I saw the tigers, like you said. But when I moved farther to the left, there was a man looking right back at me."

"Oh, man," CJ gasped. "Are you sure?"

"As sure as I'm looking at you right this minute."

"I want to go home," Jessica cried.

"Me, too," Sarah added.

"And another thing. Up till now those planes have only been coming up here in the dark. What would make them fly up on a bright, clear day like this? And how come they flew right over where we were? I tell you, I could almost smell the coffee that one pilot was drinking."

"What about our fort?"

"What about it?"

"They're going to know we've been out here in the woods spying on them."

"They don't need a dumb fort to figure that out. I might as well have sent them an email saying, 'Hey. Over here. Can you see me? Good.' That man can recognize me. What if he comes to the store or something? What if he starts asking questions?"

"We can stay out of sight for a couple days," CJ offered.

"First thing tomorrow, we have to tear down the fort and scatter the logs. After that, we can think about a plan."

"What about your dad's telescope?"

"Don't anybody say a word about it. I'll think of something."

Chapter 10

The cousins were unusually quiet at dinner that night. It was difficult to accept what they had been through, but to try and tell their parents about it seemed impossible.

"Could you kids make a little less noise?" Uncle Joe joked. "I can't hear myself chew."

"I know," Andy's father added. "What's wrong with you anyway?"

"Nothing, Dad."

"Yeah, we're just a little tired, that's all," CJ added.

"Well, I have a great idea!"

"What?" Andy asked.

"It's such a clear night. The moon is out, so I thought we could dust off the ol' telescope, and I can show you some of the constellations."

Andy's entire body went completely stiff with fear. As if the man with binoculars wasn't bad enough, this was ten times worse.

"So what do you think?"

CJ nervously cleared his throat. "I have an even better idea."

"What's that?"

"Why don't we, um, play gray wolf?"

"That's a great idea," Jessica squealed.

"How do you play gray wolf? I forget," Sarah said.

Relieved, Andy told her, "You remember, we've played it up here before."

"Well, somebody explain the rules to me again."

"We will, once we get back outside."

The families finished the rest of their dinner, including dessert. Andy even felt a little better. He tried to forget that face, those eyes.

After the dishes were cleared away, the children went outside with their fathers.

Andy's dad explained the rules and the boundaries. "This chair I've brought out will be the goal. It's the only safe place in all of Canada for gray wolf players. Once you touch it, you're safe until the next round. If the wolf touches you, you become the next wolf. If everyone makes it back to the goal without being caught, then the wolf in that round will be the wolf again for the next round."

"Hey, Sarah," CJ asked. "How come you're wearing a white shirt?"

"Jessie's is white, too."

"Oh, yeah, it is."

"Can you wait till we go change, Dad?" Sarah pleaded.

"Sure. Otherwise you might as well carry lanterns so the wolf can see you even better." Everyone else laughed at that idea. The girls ran to their cabins, changed into dark clothes, and hurried back. Andy, CJ, and their fathers wore dark sweatshirts.

"Okay, who wants to be the first wolf?"

"Nobody wants to be the wolf, Dad," Andy complained.

"Since you answered the question, you're it."

"Hey, no fair."

"Life's not fair, Andy. Now remember, you have to turn your back to us and count to twenty-five. We can hide anywhere we want to. Then you have to try and catch at least one of us, so that you get to hide the next time."

"I know how to play, Dad."

"Here are the boundaries. No one can go behind the cabins. You can hide in the rocks and trees from that big tree there on the left and over to the other big one to my right. Draw an imaginary line between them and don't go farther out than that. Any questions?"

"Yeah, are you guys still here?" Andy groaned.

"All right. Count!" With that, the other five ran for cover. Andy's dad quickly climbed into a tree. Jessica and Sarah hid behind the same big rock. No one was sure where CJ went. Uncle Joe hid behind the biggest tree he could find. The moon gave the wolf a definite advantage. Once his eyes had adjusted to the dark, Andy was able to make out a few shapes around the two areas beyond their cabins.

"Twenty-two . . . twenty-three . . . twenty-four . . . twenty-five. Ready or not, here I come!"

It was a good thing the girls changed into darker clothes.

They would have stood out like lampposts in the white shirts they first had on. Andy slipped into the shadows and hid there like a cat hunting at night. He got into the position like the fourth man in a relay, just waiting for his turn to break out running at full speed. As he dug one of his shoes into the soft ground, a dark form streaked right past him.

"Free!" Uncle Joe called out. Then from directly behind him, his father and CJ ran past on the other side. They made it to the goal too. *I should at least be able to catch one of the girls*, he thought. But they didn't move from behind their rock. Then Andy got an idea.

"Hey, there's that scary man from the lodge!"

Both girls screamed so loudly, they fell backwards into the sand. All Andy had to do was run behind the rock and have his pick of the next wolf. "Gotcha, Sarah. You're it."

"That was the dirtiest trick you've ever pulled

on me. I should tell." The three of them dashed back to the goal to start the next round.

"Sarah's it."

"Yeah, but Andy cheated."

"You can't cheat in gray wolf. Unless you go outside the boundaries, there are no rules," her father told her. She took her position near the goal with her back to the playing area. Then Sarah started counting. "One . . . two . . . three." The others disappeared into the darkness again. This time they all climbed trees and hid in the branches. Sarah finished counting, turned around, and headed out to catch somebody, anybody. Andy watched as she looked all over the place, but couldn't find one Washburn. She began walking back toward the goal like she was about ready to call out, "I give up," when someone coughed.

"Who was that?" she asked.

"Just one of us trees."

Sarah began looking into all the trees near her until something shiny caught her eye. "You're it," she called out.

"No, I'm not," CJ complained. "You have to tag me first."

"I do not. All I have to do is see you, and I see you. You're it. CJ is it!"

"That's not fair," he complained.

"No rules, remember?" Sarah taunted.

"Next wolf has to tag," Uncle Joe instructed.

They continued playing the game until each person had been the wolf at least once. It was getting colder and time for bed. Andy was glad CJ had thought about playing the game. It saved his hide, he figured, for now.

"Thanks, man. I think my dad forgot all about his telescope."

"Let's hope it stays that way," CJ cautioned. "Tomorrow just you and me should go out and see if we can find a hole in the fence."

"You crazy? I don't want to go near that place," Andy cautioned.

"You read the same thing I did about telling people if we see any poachers. Well, we *did* see them."

"Yeah, and don't forget, one of them saw me, too."

"Seeing us could make them nervous. If they think we know what they're up to, those guys might pull up and move out of the area."

"So?"

"They'll just set up some place else. These are bad people. They belong in prison."

"I guess you're right, only I have a bad feeling about going over there."

"So do I, but we have to be sure."

"When you get up in the morning, wear stuff that's green and brown." Andy told him.

"Why?"

"So we can blend into the woods like army guys."

"Okay. If you say so."

Andy didn't sleep well that night. He kept seeing himself creeping close to the lodge, only to be caught by that scary man with the black beard and the big scar on his forehead He'd seen him close up. Every time Andy closed his eyes he saw that face. Finally, he went to sleep. His cousin had to wake him the next morning.

"Andy, get up."

"What time is it?"

"Eight. Our parents went fishing, and the girls are picking blueberries. After that, they're just going to play in my cabin. It's a perfect time to get outta here. We can grab some food in the kitchen and eat on the run."

CJ wore brown pants and a green shirt. Andy searched around till he found clothes that looked about the same. They filled a paper bag with food and slipped out the back door.

CJ munched on a blueberry muffin. "Okay, use your direction finder. We need to look for a place where we can go through the fence."

"I'll find the fence, but I can't promise a way through. The only thing it's missing is a bunch of guard towers and searchlights like a prison break movie. You got your digital camera?"

CJ tapped his pocket. "Right here."

Off they ran toward the place Andy remembered seeing the fence earlier. It didn't take long till they were standing right next to it again.

"We should have brought leather gloves so we could go over the top," CJ noted.

"Well, we didn't. I wonder how old this thing is?"

"Why do you care?" CJ asked.

"If it's new, then there's no way."

"And?"

"If it's been here for awhile, there might be a couple possibilities."

"Like what?"

"Like where a heavy tree fell on it in a storm or a bear might have dug under it."

"Wait a minute. Did you say a bear?"

"Okay then, a wolf."

"That's no better."

"Any animal then. Is that okay?"

"Much better. Let's go."

The boys found the place where they had first discovered the fence. "Let's try up this way," Andy pointed. They walked farther back into the woods until they came to a place where the fence made a corner. Way up high a white sign with red warning letters that said, "No trespassing. Violators will be arrested."

"These people are serious," CJ whispered.

"I think we should go back where we came from,

and then try following the fence toward the lake," Andy suggested.

"You're the one who knows where we are. I'm following you." The boys turned and went the other way and walked for over an hour.

"I've never seen a fence this long, have you?" CJ asked.

"Never." Then Andy saw something. "Get down," he ordered.

"What is it?"

"Look down there." He pointed to a gate in the fence. Leading through it were a series of small tire tracks. "Remember those guys riding in the woods when we first came out here?"

"Oh, yeah. I do."

"I think we can squeeze through where the gate is held by that chain."

"It looks like just enough room," CJ said.

Like the tigers they had seen in cages, the boys slipped quietly through the trees, being careful not to make a sound. When they came to the gate, Andy held it so his cousin could push through. Then CJ did the same for Andy. "Now what?" CJ asked.

"Let's follow these tracks and see where they go." The boys walked cautiously along a rough trail the men had made with their ATV's.

"It's so quiet back here," CJ whispered.

"Let's make sure we keep it that way," Andy cautioned.

The trail snaked through thick woods until it came to a small hill. When the boys reached the top, they had a clear view of the lodge.

Andy studied the layout. "If we go into the gully over there, it looks like we can make it clear up to that first shed without anyone seeing us."

They crept down into the ditch and carefully walked over rocks and fallen branches until they were almost to the lake. "Let's try up there," Andy pointed. He and his cousin found a place at the top of the ridge where they could hide behind a fallen tree. CJ took out his camera.

"That thing has a zoom, doesn't it?" Andy asked.

"I'm testing it for my dad's company. There isn't anything it can't do."

"Great. Start shooting."

"Shooting what?"

"Anything you see. Animals . . . people . . . anything!" CJ began snapping digital pictures of the activities around the lodge.

"I'm not positive, but it looks like they're packing up to leave."

"Really?" Andy asked.

"Here. I have it zoomed all the way in. See what you think."

Andy took the camera and started scanning

the grounds. He saw a stack of cages. Each one had some kind of bird or furry animal in it. Many of the cages were small, but there were about a dozen that were quite large. "They're either getting ready to ship a bunch of stuff, or you're right. They could be leaving."

"We gotta do something!"

No sooner did he say those words, than the boys began to hear the sounds of barking dogs. The noise got louder by the second.

"Guard dogs!" Andy gasped. "Let's move it!"

The boys turned and ran back up the gully toward the gate. For a few seconds the dogs didn't seem as loud. Then Andy turned to look back. He wished he hadn't done that. A pack of vicious looking dogs were rushing down the side of the ditch and running straight toward them. "I don't care how fast you *think* you're running, CJ, we have to go faster!"

The boys strained to pick up speed. The gully went slightly up hill making their legs begin to ache. But the dogs were getting louder. Worse than that, it meant they were coming closer, too.

"I see the gate!" Andy yelled.

They had no time to hold it for each other, but that didn't really matter. They hit the small opening with such force each boy shot right through it and tumbled onto the ground, safe on the other side. Andy jumped up, grabbed a stick, and wedged it between the gate and the fence so the dogs couldn't get through.

"Whew. I thought they were going to eat my face off." Andy said breathlessly.

"What's *that* sound?" CJ cried.

"Run!" Andy knew what it was. The same men on the ATV's they'd seen before were now searching for them. "Run, CJ, Run!" Tears streamed down Andy's cheeks. Never in his life had he been so scared.

Chapter 11

Somehow they made it back safely to Andy's cabin. At the same time and only about 100 yards away, the men drove up to the small store. They stopped there, and went inside. From the security of their cabin the boy's could watch the store.

"Do you think they're looking for us?"

"I know it," Andy answered.

After only a few minutes, the men came back outside. They began walking in one direction but quickly returned to the front of the store. They repeated this at least twice, each time going off in another direction.

It looked to Andy like they were asking questions of everyone they found. He watched as a man pointed back toward the woods. Another pointed right at Andy's cabin. Andy ducked down behind the curtain. Then, suddenly, the back door slowly began to open. The hinges made an eerie sound. The door slammed shut like a shotgun. Andy and his cousin fell to the floor like dead men.

"Hey, you guys wanna come out and play?"

Jessica asked as she and Sarah walked in.

"You almost gave us a heart attack," Andy complained.

"How come?"

"Did you see all those guys ride in here a few minutes ago?"

"Yeah . . . from the woods. Who are they?"

"They're from the lodge, and they are . . . uh . . . looking for us!"

"What for?" Sarah asked.

"Because we sneaked through their fence," Andy told her.

"And I took a bunch of pictures," CJ added hoarsely.

"Show us."

CJ turned on his camera so they could view the pictures. When the girls were finished, Sarah sighed sadly, "Those poor animals."

"I know," her brother said, "and we plan to do something about it."

"We do?" CJ asked.

"Yes, I just don't know what yet."

Their parents would be back from fishing soon, and Andy had an idea. "CJ, in your box of junk, do you have what it would take to build a radio transmitter?"

"What kind of transmitter?"

"One of those things like big airplanes have when

they crash in the water so divers can find them."

"You mean like a locator? Sure. That'd be simple with a couple of the things I brought for another project I'm already building."

"Then go to your cabin and make it."

"Right now?"

"Yes."

"But those guys. . ."

"Just be careful. Now go." CJ slinked across to his cabin being careful so no one would see him. The girls went back out to play. CJ was back in his cabin making the transmitter when Andy heard a knock at the front door. He decided to pretend like nobody was home. The only problem is the door began to open anyway. Andy scooted under the bed in his parent's room just as someone came through the front door. He didn't know who it was. All he could see were a pair of dirty, black boots on someone who walked into the bedroom, passing only inches from his head. He watched as they came to a stop, turned, then left the room. The next sound he heard was the front door slamming.

This is not good, he thought. When it seemed safe again, he rolled out from under the bed and, crouching down, made his way over to the front window of the cabin. He looked out just in time to see the men riding their all terrain vehicles back toward the woods.

Andy darted toward the front door, but it blew open like it had been hit by a blast of North wind, right off the lake. On the other side, CJ was about to run in. He stopped. The boys looked at each other. Then they both screamed as loud as two boys can scream. Andy turned to run under the bed again when his cousin realized what was happening. "Andy. Wait up. It's just me." Then both boys began to laugh nervously.

"We need to come up with a plan for tonight," Andy told him.

"You got any ideas?" CJ asked.

"A couple."

"Fire away."

"I saw one of those two-man rubber boats tied to the dock the other day."

"The little black one?"

"That's it."

"I saw it, too. It has it's own paddles and everything."

"Right. Whoever owns it probably won't miss the thing if we take it out just for the night."

"Okay, then what?" CJ asked.

"We dress up in the darkest clothes we own, put black stuff from the fireplace on our hands and faces, take your transmitter, glue a couple refrigerator magnets to the back of it, and see if we can stick it on one of their planes."

"Two problems, cousin."

"What are they?"

"Well, first, there aren't any planes over there, and second, even if there were, planes are made of aluminum."

"The planes are coming back. Trust me. Those guys are packing up to leave. So, what if planes are made out of aluminum?"

"Magnets won't stick to aluminum."

"Oh, that's right. Well, most of the floats have little doors in the top."

"They do? How come?" CJ asked.

"I saw a guy down at the dock the other day. He had a little hand pump he was turning."

"Go on."

"So, I asked him what he was doing. He told me that most floats start leaking after a lot of landings on the water. Every so often the pilot has to get that water out, so he uses a pump to take it out from the top."

"What's your idea?"

"First, you hook the transmitter up with some of your super long-life batteries. That thing will be singing for weeks. Then we put it in triple plastic bags so it won't get wet."

"Smart," CJ complimented.

"My idea is smart, but I'm not so sure you're going to like the rest of it."

North Woods Poachers

"How do we put the transmitter into one of the floats?" CJ asked.

"We can't go through the fence again," Andy warned. "Those dogs would use us for chew toys. So we synchronize our watches, then wait till our parents and our sisters are asleep. I figure around eleven. We'll set our watches so at exactly eleven o'clock, we can slip out the windows of our bedrooms. We can meet by your dad's truck."

"Then what?" CJ asked.

"Then we go down to the dock."

"I knew you were going to say that."

"We go to the dock," Andy repeated, "pull the rubber boat up on shore, and carry it as far as Rocky Point. From there we'll have to get in and paddle over to their dock."

"Sounds good so far. No dogs."

"While I steer us up beside the planes, you drop that little baby into one of the floats, and we just head back where we came from."

"What if the planes don't come tonight?"

"If you're right, and they don't, we can use this as a test run. But I'm telling you, something's coming. I can just feel it."

"But the plan's still no good," CJ complained.

"Why not?"

"Well, we haven't told anyone yet."

"After we come back, we'll have to get on the

computer and contact that web site we found. We can make the report to them. They'll know what to do."

"Great. I think this is going to work. I mean, what could go wrong?"

"Plenty. It's best if we don't think about that and just concentrate on what had *better* go right."

Their parents came home from another full day on the water, just as the sun was going down. Andy and his cousin tried to act as if nothing was wrong. Andy was glad they couldn't see inside his head because it was filled with some terrible pictures.

The families ate their usual big dinner together, but the parents were so tired from the sun, they wanted to go to bed early. "Try to be quiet," Andy's mother said. "We're really worn out."

"Okay, Mom." This was perfect. Andy went over to CJ and whispered, "We can move it up to nine-thirty. There should still be a little light, and our sisters will be in bed by then anyway."

"I think you're right. Once the sun goes down up here, and since we don't have lights, I get pretty tired, too."

"Well, this time, we have to stay awake."

"I will."

"Let's check our watches. Set yours to exactly seven-thirty on my mark . . . mark!"

"See you at nine-thirty," CJ promised.

North Woods Poachers

"See you!"

CJ and his sister went back to their cabin. For all the families knew, this would be just another night up North. But it wouldn't be. Even Andy hadn't planned as well as he should have for what was coming next.

At exactly nine twenty-eight, he slipped out of his bed. After he made sure his sister was well into her third dream, he lifted the window, tossed out his shoes, then slipped outside, closing the window behind him. CJ came silently around the corner. If it hadn't been for his face and hands, Andy might never have seen him. Clouds had moved in, completely covering the moon.

"Here," Andy offered, handing his cousin some charcoal from the fireplace.

"Thanks. I forgot about that part."

They took a few minutes to smear the black soot onto each other's faces and necks. Then they each did their own hands.

"You look like the potbelly stove blew up in your face," Andy joked.

"Looks like you were standing next to me when it did."

"That's it," Andy declared. "Time to go."

Quietly the boys crept toward the dock. They made sure no one could see them. A woman came out of one cabin, but she went around the back of it and never saw Andy or CJ. But just to be sure, they hid behind trees until she was out of sight. They quickly made their way to the dock and found the little boat. CJ untied the rope and pulled it up to where Andy was waiting on the shore. Since it was made of rubber and filled with air, the small boat was easy for them to carry. Each boy took one of the paddles, and they were on their way.

The sky gave off a dull gray glow as the sun set behind the darkening blanket of clouds. Soon it was dark out. When they reached Rocky Point, it was time to put the boat into the water, climb in, and push off from the safety of the water's edge. Suddenly, Andy wasn't convinced that his plan was such a good one after all, but it was too late. The junior investigators were already far out into the still water. It was so still and quiet that the only noise they heard came from the sound their paddles made moving through the water.

Then it happened. Andy heard it first, and as he turned his head to look, CJ heard it, too. "What . . . what in the world?" he asked.

"I don't know. Shhh. . ." Andy cautioned. It was a sound unlike anything they had heard on this trip or any other. At first, they could make out a low rumble in the distance.

"Thunder storm?" CJ asked. "Because you aren't

supposed to be out here if there's lightning."

"It isn't thunder."

"What then?"

"I think it's something else."

At that instant the sound broke through the cloud cover, and along with it came flashing lights . . .big ones. If that wasn't bad enough, headlights, blinding headlights, came on, making it impossible for the boys to look at them.

"It's an airplane, CJ . . . a big jet."

"They're going to crash right into the lake. I know they are," CJ cried.

Chapter 12

Andy wasn't sure if they should stay where they were. What if the giant plane was about to take them with it to the bottom? Then it made a slow turn as the engines became even louder.

"Maybe they just dropped under the clouds to see where they were," CJ hoped out loud.

"Well, then I don't think that was much help because I doubt they could see a thing."

The large jet didn't climb back into the clouds. Instead, it continued to make a big circle until it lined up the same way the other black floatplanes had before.

Andy watched in amazement. "I think they're going to. . . land!"

"On the *water*? Are you completely crazy?"

"No, look. It's leveling off and dropping toward the water."

"Jets don't land on water," CJ protested. "Do they?"

"Looks like this one does." Andy noticed it was also painted completely black. As it touched down on the water, there was such a thunderous roar both boys had to cover their ears. Water sprayed far out behind the powerful jet engines moving the plane along the water.

CJ pointed. "It's headed for the lodge."

"Big surprise," Andy said. "Come on. Start paddling."

"Are you nuts? I'm for going back."

"We can't stop now."

"But Andy, this is way too big for just us. We need the National Guard."

"This is Canada. Our National Guard doesn't come up here."

"Then the Mounties! Come on! Bring in some serious troops. Something . . . anything . . . I don't care what."

"Start paddling!"

From where they were in the water, the boys had a clear view of the lodge now. The dark plane seemed to settle about halfway into the water. It slowly made its way toward the dock at the lodge. The boys continued moving in that direction, too. Andy suddenly noticed big searchlights moving back and forth along the beach and the fence-line, but not out into the water. *That's a break*, he thought.

"Those dummies probably didn't think anyone would be stupid enough to come in this way," CJ whispered. "Man, they don't know what real dummies look like."

"I wonder if that thing woke up our parents?" Andy asked.

When the rubber boat was only a few hundred feet from the jet, the boys could see cages already being loaded into a large door that had opened on the side of the plane opposite from where they were. People moved quickly around the lodge while the boys continued to slip silently through the water.

"I hope you're right about floats having doors on top," CJ whispered.

"Me, too. I wasn't counting on something that's almost as long as a football field." They noticed that there was no activity at all on their side of the airplane. No one stood guard and no searchlights came out toward them. The boys were able to paddle safely, right up to one of the gigantic floats.

Andy reached out to catch it so they didn't make a sound. "Check out your transmitter. Make sure it's working."

CJ switched it on. "Perfect," he smiled.

"You have to get out of the boat and look for a door."

"Why can't *you* do that?" he whispered.

"Just do it," Andy demanded. "I'll hold the boat."

"Well, don't hurt yourself," CJ sneered. He climbed out onto the float and began feeling for an opening . . . any opening. Just then one of the men walked around from the back of the airplane. He stood there for a moment, looked out over the black water, then he left without seeing the boys or their little boat. *Man that was close,* Andy thought.

CJ continued inching his way along the length of the massive float. When he reached one of the supports, his hand ran across something that made him stop. Andy wondered if anything was wrong, but as he watched, it looked like his cousin opened a door. The next thing he heard was a small thump. *Must have dropped it in,* he thought.

CJ returned and slipped back into the boat. "Let's get out of here."

As silently as they had come, the boys began paddling away. Just as they were about to go around Rocky Point, something terrible happened. It felt like every searchlight at the lodge pointed directly at them.

"Paddle your arms off, CJ. They've seen us!" And paddle they did which was a good thing because they heard several jet skis fire up. With their headlights blazing, the watercraft began heading toward the boys in their pitiful little rubber boat.

"They're gonna catch us for sure," CJ cried.

"Not a chance. Now paddle!" Even Andy was surprised how fast they made it to the other side of the point. When they got there, the boys leaped out of the boat, pulled it into some tall grass, and ran back toward their cabins as fast as they could.

"I have to get to my computer so we can email that wildlife place."

The boys went to CJ's cabin and climbed in his window. They gathered up his computer equipment and headed out the back door. As they did that, the men on jet skis continued searching the waters all along the shoreline. CJ connected everything, then started the generator. He'd forgotten what a loud noise it made so he stopped it right away. "Help me put this thing in the back of my dad's truck. Together they lifted the generator up there. Then he started it again. This time, it wasn't nearly so loud.

CJ went on the Internet, called up his favorite files, scrolled down to the address for the wildlife organization, and clicked on it. Up popped the web page. Quickly he searched for the contact information and found it. He clicked on that, and an email page came up. "What should I say?" CJ asked.

"Type this," Andy began. "Dear wildlife people.

This is not a joke, even if what we tell you sounds like one. My cousin and I read on your site that if we see anything suspicious about animals, we should tell someone. Well, we have, and we are.

"We're at Dore Lake, way up in Canada. You probably don't know where it is. We came up here to go fishing. Well, we caught some fish all right, but if you come up here right away, you're gonna catch something bigger.

"My cousin and I found some people at an abandoned lodge. They kept bringing in float-planes just before dark, and they'd leave the next morning just before the sun came up. So we went to investigate.

"We found lots of animals and birds in cages. We got chased by dogs, men on ATV's, and again on jet skis tonight. But that was nothing because some men at the lodge saw us watching them from a fire tower through our telescope.

"Anyway, tonight a big float-plane came in and landed on Dore Lake. It wasn't just any float-plane. This one was a jet, a great big one. The men are loading it with their animals now, so if you don't get up here right away, they'll be gone by daylight, like they always are. Then you won't be able to catch them.

"Please hurry!

"Your friends,

"Andy & CJ

"Oh, one more thing. My cousin built a transmitter and we went over there tonight and put it in one of the big plane's floats and here's a picture of some of the animals."

"They aren't going to believe any of this. You know that." CJ sighed. Then he hit send.

Just then a loud voice demanded, "What are you boys doing out here?"

Andy thought they were dead, but CJ recognized his father's voice right away. "Hi, Dad! You won't believe this."

"Believe what?"

"We'd better get my dad too," Andy cautioned.

CJ shut everything off before they ran back toward the cabins. CJ's mother was standing on the porch. "What in the world?" she asked.

"Come on. We all have to get inside before they see us," Andy warned them.

"Before *who* sees us?"

"We'll tell you inside after I get my parents. Don't light any lamps. I'll be right back, but get inside, please!" Andy ran to his cabin and pounded on the window to his parent's bedroom.

"Dad. Mom. Get up." His father came over and opened the window. "What do you have on your face?" he demanded.

"I'll tell you over at Uncle Joe's cabin. Hurry,

and bring Sarah with you."

Andy's parents looked worried as they came through the door. Sarah was crying. "What is that awful stuff on your face, Andy?" she asked.

"I know. It must look pretty scary. Well, actually it is scary!"

"What is going on?" his father demanded.

"It's a long story, Dad."

"Well, why don't you give us the short version then."

"You're always telling me to do the right thing. Right?"

"Go on."

"Well, sort of by accident, the four of us thought we saw some poachers over at the old lodge."

"But we told you not to go near that place."

"We didn't. Not at first," CJ told them.

"No. At first we were only exploring a big fire tower out in the woods . . . from the top of the ladder."

"You climbed to the top of a fire tower?" Aunt Julie demanded. "Even the girls?"

"Yes, Mom," Jessica said proudly.

"Anyway, from up there we saw them with your telescope."

"My what?"

"Your telescope. We took it up there. Only when I was looking around, I was suddenly staring right into the face of a man who was staring back at me."

"Then we went through the fence, and dogs chased us, and we borrowed a boat and went over to the lodge where a great big jet landed on the water."

Aunt Julie yawned. "I thought that was only thunder."

"Wait a minute! Wait just a minute. When does doing the right thing start?" Uncle Joe asked. "So far all I've heard has been about some children who did all the wrong things."

"I know that now, Dad."

Then CJ started again. "We got chased by guys on ATV's. They came to the store and asked people a bunch of questions."

"One even came into our cabin," Andy added. "So I hid under the bed."

"Okay! I've heard enough! First thing in the morning, we have to call someone," Andy's father said.

"We sort of already did that. We were just finishing when you came out and found us by your truck."

"Who did you tell?"

"We aren't exactly sure, but we emailed a wildlife web site that asked people to report stuff like this."

"But those men could have caught you, or

worse," Andy's mother cautioned.

"I know, Mom. Only, if you'd seen those poor animals, what would you have done?"

"That's not the point. You really should have told us."

"Then you wouldn't have let us do what we did."

"Don't expect anyone to come. I doubt if they believed your email," Andy's father said.

Andy sighed. "Yeah. That's what we think, too. But we had to try."

"So you're saying that some men might be looking for you right now?"

"I *know* they are because they shined their searchlights right on us just before we made it around Rocky Point. That's when the guys on jet skis started chasing us."

"Well, I'm sort of proud of you boys and sort of angry with you all at the same time," Andy's father told them. "I'm just glad you're all right. Let's all sleep in this cabin tonight.

That way, if anything happens, at least we'll be together."

It seemed to Andy as if morning came faster than usual. Of course, he hadn't gotten to bed until nearly three o'clock in the morning. He didn't wake up because he'd gotten enough sleep. Andy heard something.

Chapter 13

"Come on," Andy yelled. "Let's go to the dock."

The families followed, and at the dock they found other people already standing there.

"What's that noise? What's happening?" others asked.

Another man walked up and stopped by the edge of the lake. "Didn't anyone hear it last night?"

"We heard something, but it was dark out."

"I thought it was going to crash, only I couldn't see anything," a woman answered.

As the crowd strained to see what was making all that racket, the great jet Andy and CJ had seen the night before, made its way out from Rocky Point.

"What is that thing?" a man asked.

"It's a jet," Andy told him.

"Jets don't land on water."

Andy pointed toward the plane. "Well, that one does." Slowly, the low rumble changed into a defining roar. Water sprayed like a hurricane from the blast of its powerful engines. The plane began to pick up speed until it was skimming across the early morning calm of Dore Lake. Then, to the amazement of everyone standing there, except Andy and CJ, it gently lifted into the air and was gone in just a few seconds.

"Your poachers got away," Sarah said.

"It might look like it, but maybe they haven't."

"What poachers are you kids talking about?" the storekeeper asked.

"That's what they've been doing over at the old lodge. Poaching."

"Poaching what?"

"All kinds of wild animals and birds, that's what. They bring them in with the two black planes."

"But you have no proof," Uncle Joe reasoned.

"We have proof!" Andy shot back.

"What kind of proof?"

Before CJ could run to get his camera and show the digital pictures to his father, the people on the dock got another big surprise. Suddenly, like mosquitoes in July, the early morning sky was filled with a swarm of high-speed float-planes that swooped in from all directions. They began landing on the water and all of them headed toward the docks.

"What is going on here?" a woman asked.

The storekeeper rubbed his hands together with delight. "I'm going to sell so much gas and sandwiches today!" He ran to his store to get ready.

Andy's father continued. "Looks like help came a little too late. Those guys got away clean."

"I don't think so, Dad."

"Why not?"

"Tell them, CJ."

"I made a radio transmitter. Me and Andy went over there and dropped it inside one of the floats on that big jet.

After they took off this morning, if anyone is trying to find them, all they have to do is tune in to the frequency. Here, I wrote it down." He handed the paper to his father.

Just then a very large man stepped out of the first floatplane that came to the dock. He walked up to the group of people that was getting larger every minute. The man pulled an electronic organizer out of his jacket pocket, took out the stylist pen, and touched the screen. "Is there anyone here by the names of Andy and CJ?" he asked.

Both boys tried to slip behind their fathers.

"Here they are, officer," Uncle Joe announced.

"Thanks a lot, Dad," CJ complained.

"Let's go someplace quiet. I'd like to talk with

you boys for a minute."

"Our cabins are right this way," Andy's father offered.

Once inside, the man started, "I've spent a lot of money getting here this morning . . . you saw all of my men and equipment. If your email was a hoax, you boys are in more trouble than I can tell you."

"No, sir. It's true," Andy said proudly.

"Then I need more proof."

"CJ, go get it." His cousin bolted from the cabin and returned with his digital camera. When he went to turn on the power, nothing happened.

"I thought you said you had all the batteries we needed."

"We do. I'll be right back."

Again he darted out of the cabin. This time he brought back a box with dozens of different batteries. Rummaging through them he complained, "Where are they? Where are they? There!" He pulled out batteries, opened the battery compartment on his camera, let the dead ones drop to the floor, and quickly inserted fresh ones. This time when he turned the switch, the camera came right on. Then, one by one, CJ began displaying each image.

"They'd look much better if I hooked up to my laptop," he offered.

"It's okay. Just keep going."

"Oh, that one is so sad," Andy's mother said

when she saw one of the big cats.

"But they got away," Uncle Joe grumbled.

Just then there was a knock at the front door. Another officer came in and whispered something into the big man's ear then went back outside again.

"I have good news for you. But first I have a question."

"What's that, officer?" Andy's father asked.

"Whose idea was it to put a bug in the plane, and how did you do it?"

"Listen," Andy responded nervously, "we had nothing to do with any bugs. Those guys must have loaded them in there by themselves."

The big man chuckled. "No, no. Not insects. I mean the locator signal. That thing started singing as soon as they were airborne."

"I did that, sir," CJ said sheepishly.

"One of the best pieces of detective work I've ever seen. And I've been doing this job for a lot a years." He slapped his hand on his knee and started laughing.

"But I didn't tell anyone the frequency," CJ protested.

"Son," the man began, "we have every kind of electronic scanning equipment you can imagine."

"Boy, would I ever like to see that."

"Keep working on electronics like you're doing now and one day you might wanna come to work for me."

"Really?"

"The other officer who was just here has been on the radio relaying information to some of our people. The minute that jet crossed into US airspace, a couple of their fighter jets forced it to the nearest airbase."

"But I thought it could only land on water."

"No, sir. It's an amphibian. The Russians developed them for use in Siberia. That bird is just as comfortable on land as it is on water."

Andy shook his head. "No kidding? How about that."

"Listen. I've got some details to take care of. Give me your addresses. We'll be in touch with you later. We're going to send a joint US-Canadian team in to search for more evidence at the lodge." He turned to the boys. "Fine job. Fine job." Then he went out the door. Andy could still hear him laughing.

He and his cousin wanted to see what would happen next, but it wasn't what they expected. The big man walked back to his float-plane, climbed in, and shut the door. The engine turned over. One after another the planes that had swooped in were ready for take off. They turned out toward the open water and in minutes all of them lifted off into the sky.

"I think this is the biggest thing that's ever happened," CJ said as they walked on to the dock.

The storekeeper came running down from his store carrying a large cardboard box. "Oh, no! Where are they going?

I made all these sandwiches. And they didn't even buy one drop of gas. Oh, this is terrible I tell you, simply terrible."

The boys only grinned at each other. "I wonder how the animals are doing?" CJ asked.

"It has to be better than some of the places they could have gone."

"I guess so. I'm glad we have the pictures to remember." CJ said.

"Pictures? I thought you gave your whole camera to that animal guy."

"I did."

"Then what are you talking about?"

"After we took them the other day, I downloaded all the pictures to my hard drive. You can have as many as you want."

"You are really something, you know that?"

"I know," CJ, said with a smile. "I know."

A few days later, a letter came by special messenger. Andy's father had to sign for it. When he brought it in he said, "It's addressed to *Andy and C J: Special Agents.*"

"Does it really say 'Special Agents'?"

"Right there after your names."

"Wait a minute. Let me get CJ so we can open it together."

"Tell the rest of the family, too," his father called out.

"I will!" Andy stormed out the front door. In seconds he and his cousin were back. It took a little longer for CJ's parents to get there.

"Now, we can start," Andy's dad announced.

Andy quickly tore open the envelope. His hands were shaking so bad he begged, "Here. You read it, Dad."

"Dear Agents."

"It really says that?" Uncle Joe asked.

"Right here." He pointed to the words at the top of the letter.

"Keep reading," Aunt Julie pleaded.

"I wanted to send our appreciation on behalf of the joint task force and to let you know how BIG your discovery actually was."

By this time Andy and his cousins' faces beamed.

"After the plane was diverted to the US air base, we captured twenty poachers and a large quantity of animals, birds, weapons, and equipment."

"Weapons?" Andy's mother asked.

Sarah put her finger over her lips. "Shhh. . . ."

"I've included two lists of all the animals and equipment; one for each of you."

"Let me see that," CJ said. "Man, I had no idea there could be that much."

"Our agents at the old lodge confiscated several vehicles and more equipment the poachers were either too lazy to load on the plane or that they thought might make it too heavy to lift off the water. The most important find was their computer."

CJ groaned, "Give me ten minutes with that thing and I'd have cracked this case open like a walnut."

"Their electronic records included a list of their suppliers along with all of the places where they sent shipments over the past five years. Our agents worldwide are making more arrests even as I write this letter to you."

"Think of it," Andy said. "One minute you're asleep in your bed in some country a million miles away, and all of a sudden, guys come to your door and take you to jail."

The letter continued, *"By the time you return to your homes, you will find two certificates that I took the liberty of having framed for you. One is for bravery . . . that comes from my department. The other is a thank you, and it comes on behalf of several wildlife organizations. You boys are known around the world."*

"This is so exciting!" Jessica squealed.

"So again, thank you for your excellent detective work.

Sincerely, Agent Jackson.

"*P.S. CJ, your transmitter is sitting on my desk right now sending out its powerful signal. I still can't get over that. I'll ship it after you get home.*"

It took at least the next two or three days for everything to sink in. Even then the boys didn't have a total understanding of how big the operation they uncovered had been. Now, with nothing more to investigate, they were getting a little bored.

Andy and his cousin were sitting on stumps in the back yard when Andy's father walked up. "Hi, guys. Whatcha doing?"

"Nothin'."

"That's how it looked to me, too."

"Everything fun and exciting is over. We might as well pack up and head home," CJ complained.

"That's what I came back to tell you."

Andy sat straight up. "Yeah?"

"Uncle Joe and I thought it would be a good idea if the four of us went fishing one more time tomorrow."

"Fishing?" the boys groaned together.

Chapter 14

Very early the next morning the four were out on the lake heading to Andy's father's favorite fishing spot. The cousins had tried to avoid it as long as possible, but they knew this day was coming sometime. The lake was unusually calm. The only wind came from the speed of the boat skimming through the water. Their wake made the only waves.

In time, they reached the other side of the lake where their boat slowed, then came to a stop.

"I know the drill, Dad," CJ said as he went for the anchor and threw it out.

Each person prepared his own rod and lure, and then they began casting into the water. For some strange reason, the fish weren't biting like usual. After about an hour of this, Andy's father suggested they take a break. "We want to talk with you a little anyway," he began.

"Coming out here was the best idea I've heard all week," Andy said, trying to change whatever subject his dad had in mind.

"I thought you didn't like fishing all that much."

"I don't."

"Then what?"

"We could use a little peace and quiet after all that's happened."

"All that's happened is what we wanted to talk about. First, there's no question you boys did something good . . . really good. But in order to do that, you also did some things that weren't right. You didn't tell your parents where you were going or the danger you were in. Don't ever let that happen again."

"We won't."

"Second, in order to do something good, you did something bad."

"What was that?"

"You took someone else's property without permission."

"We did?"

"The rubber boat. Remember?"

"Oh, oh," CJ thought out loud.

"What's wrong?"

"We left that boat in the grass and didn't bring it back to the dock."

"When we get back, you have to take care of that and find the owner. When you do, you'll have to apologize for stealing their boat."

"We didn't really *steal* it."

"Yes, you stole it, Andy. There are laws. You have to follow them. Because of God's laws, there is order in nature like what we enjoy around here. With people, there are man's laws. Break any law, God's or man's, and there's going to be trouble. Do you understand that?"

"Yes," Andy answered.

"I want you to know that in everything God wants justice. He loves justice and hates injustice. Those men were breaking all kinds of laws, and it looks like they were hurting some of the animals. There wasn't anything they wouldn't do to hide their poaching. You boys could have been . . . ."

CJ shrugged his shoulders. "I know. Andy and I have talked about that since it all happened. We just weren't thinking of that part."

"It's one of the most important."

"I know that . . . now."

"Uncle Joe and I have talked it over and decided what your punishment will be."

"We get punished?" Andy protested.

"Punishment can come in lots of ways. We thought that since those men scared you as badly as they did, and since you understand how wrong you were to go about things the way you did, you've probably already decided to act differently in the future."

"We sure have, Uncle Dave," CJ sighed.

"Good. Then I have a great idea. Why don't

we pull up the anchor and go to the place where I'm almost positive Big Wally might be?"

CJ grabbed the rope and quickly lifted the anchor into the boat. "What are we sitting here for?"

Andy's father fired up the engine, slipped the gear into forward, and gave the boat full power. They headed toward an area close to the cabins that Andy hadn't fished in this year. At dinner a couple times, he'd heard the parents talking about having tried it, but no one had caught the big guy.

Andy and his cousin tensed with excitement at the thought of being the one to haul that geezer in. Soon the boat slowed again, and then came to a stop in the water.

"Don't drop the anchor this time. I want to throw off his timing a little."

"You're pretty serious about this fish, aren't you, Dad?" Andy's father didn't say a word. He took off his hat and put on another one that said, "Wally." Then he picked out his best rod and reel, chose an old, wooden lure, and prepared for the catch of his life. Over the next hour and a half all four tried as hard as they could to bring in the big one. They caught and released several smaller fish but no Wally.

Then suddenly, it happened. At first Andy

thought he'd caught his line on a sunken log, so he gave it a hard pull. Well, for the first time in his life, the log pulled back ten times harder, and it kept right on pulling.

"Let your line run, son," his father instructed.

Andy was sure it would start smoking any minute, but he did as he was told. "It's about to come to the end. DAD!" he screamed. "What should I do?"

"Slowly bring it to a stop, so it doesn't snap at the end. Here, take these gloves." His father held the rod as Andy put them on. Then he took the rod back in time to stop whatever it was on the end of his line from dragging him clear to the North Pole.

The fish was so big, and he fought so hard, each person in the boat had to take turns reeling him in. "This isn't really fair," CJ complained. "There's only one of him and four of us."

"Sure," Andy's father said, "but it could be that we've got the fish of our lives on the other end of this line."

It seemed like hours as they battled with the great fish. For a while it was possible to pull him closer and closer to the boat, and then suddenly he'd run again.

"He really doesn't want to get caught, does he?"

Andy said thoughtfully.

"Kind of like those poachers," CJ added.

"Yes, but with one very big difference."

"What's that, Dad?" Andy asked.

"This fish hasn't done anything wrong. Now keep pulling."

For the first time the fish broke through the water as he jumped high into the air. When he did that, two things happened. He thrashed his head from side to side like he was trying to spit out the hook, but at the same time each person saw it. There was no mistake. There on the tail fin of that gigantic fish was a bright red tag.

"Is that who I think it is?" Andy's father gasped. Then he had to sit down for a moment.

"No *bout-a-doubt-it*," Uncle Joe teased.

Finally, they had him close enough to the side of the boat that Andy's father could get a net under their prized catch. But that was useless. The fish was too heavy and broke right through the bottom. "Quick. Andy, you keep holding him close in. Joe, you and I have to get on each side of the fish so we can lift him out. Better get your leather gloves."

The men reached cautiously into the water. Each grabbed a hold of a gill, and then slowly hoisted the fish into the boat. Andy thought they looked like two weight lifters as they strained to get him out of the water. He was still flopping around, trying everything he could to escape. But Andy clearly read the numbers on the tag, 4 . . . 1 . . . 1 . . . 2. "It's him all right. I can't believe I'm the one who brought the old rascal in!"

CJ let out a long, deep breath. "And me without my camera."

It seemed as if everyone in the boat had the same idea at the same time. They just didn't know the others felt that way too. Andy thought that since the fish really hadn't done anything to deserve being caught, it wouldn't be right to keep him. But the biggest surprise for everyone came when his father suggested, "I think we should throw him back."

Then Uncle Joe said, "Everyone at least touch him."

"Why, Dad?" CJ asked.

"Because no one will ever believe us that's why. But at least we'll know."

"Wait a minute," Andy interrupted. "Dad, you still got that permanent marker in your tackle box?"

"I think so." He rummaged around and pulled it out. "What now?"

"Let's each write our initials on the tag and today's date. Then if anyone ever does catch him again, at least they'll know we got to him first."

North Woods Poachers

"What a great idea. Hurry though. He put up a pretty good fight. We should get him back in the water, soon."

Each angler wrote his initials and gave the fish a pat on his side. Then the uncles worked together to remove the hooks from his mouth. After that, they gently eased Big Wally beneath the surface again.

"That's it then. The old boy's gone."

Just then, there was a loud thump on the bottom of the boat as the great fish slapped it with his tail. Seconds later, he appeared a few feet away. Again he slapped his massive tail and soaked every one in the boat. Then he was gone. Andy almost felt like he was going to cry. No one said a word. Andy's father started the engine and slowly turned the boat toward the docks as he took off his Wally hat.

This time, when they came in, both aunts and both sisters had decided to wait for them on the dock. "Did you catch anything?" Andy's mother asked.

"Did we catch anything?" Andy howled. "Mom, you aren't going to believe this, but we caught Big Wally!"

"You didn't!"

"We did, too!"

"Let us see him," the girls begged. "Please, please . . . PLEASE!"

"Well, where is he?" Aunt Julie asked.

After a few moments of total silence, Andy's father said, "We didn't bring him back."

"What? Why not?"

"We all decided it wouldn't be right. So we let him go."

"You didn't!" Aunt Julie said.

"I never thought I'd see the day!" Andy's mother exclaimed.

"Wait just a minute," Aunt Julie challenged. "Something's fishy here."

"That's a good one, Mom," CJ laughed. "Up here everything is fishy. I thought that's why we keep coming back."

"Exactly how big was this fish?" Aunt Cindy asked.

Both boys stretched out their arms as far as they would go without snapping off.

"Oh, I'm so sure," she chuckled.

"I should have had my camera," CJ moaned again.

Just then, the biggest fish either family had ever seen in all the years they'd been coming to the lake jumped high into the air. It did one looping back flip, then hit the water with such force, it reminded Andy of his best cannon ball at the pool back home.

Everyone turned back, looked at one another, and as the aunts asked, "Big W?" The guys just smiled back at them.

It was as if that old fish knew something about traditions, too. Andy thought it was Wally's way of saying,

"*See you next year.*

"*Same time.*

"*Same place.*"

That made Andy smile.

- The End -

CPSIA information can be obtained at www.ICGtesting.com
Printed in the USA
240796LV00001B/15/P